"Did you just kiss me?" Angie murmured against his shoulder.

"I was waking Sleeping Beauty."

Pulling away from him to stretch, she muttered, "I think you're in the wrong fairy tale, Senator. And if you think this frog is going to turn into a princess, you're way off base."

He drew her back against him and laughed softly. "Sam, remember?"

"Sure, Sam," she said, her voice sounding irritated, as memories of what had taken place before she fell asleep returned and she resented the way he had seduced her into exposing her vulnerability.

"What was that?" she said, jerking her head up as she heard the muffled sound of sliding rocks.

"We're either being rescued," he replied lazily, "or there's a gopher out there I'd prefer not to meet."

Reluctantly Angie began to laugh, feeling amusement and relief and excitement that they were finally being rescued. But she also felt a touch of regret at the inevitable loss of the camaraderie they had shared.

"Angel," Sam said, interrupting her thoughts. "Before they get here, there's something I want to know."

"Yes?" She raised her head to look up at him even though it was pitch dark, then found her lips captured by his in a soft, exploring kiss.

WHAT ARE *LOVESWEPT* ROMANCES?

They are stories of true romance and touching emotion. We believe those two very important ingredients are constants in our highly sensual and very believable stories in the *LOVESWEPT* line. Our goal is to give you, the reader, stories of consistently high quality that may sometimes make you laugh, sometimes make you cry, but are always fresh and creative and contain many delightful surprises within their pages.

Most romance fans read an enormous number of books. Those they truly love, they keep. Others may be traded with friends and soon forgotten. We hope that each *LOVESWEPT* romance will be a treasure—a "keeper." We will always try to publish

*LOVE STORIES YOU'LL NEVER FORGET
BY AUTHORS YOU'LL ALWAYS REMEMBER*

The Editors

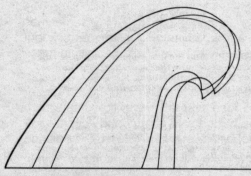

LOVESWEPT • 38

Billie Green
Temporary Angel

BANTAM BOOKS
NEW YORK • TORONTO • LONDON • SYDNEY • AUCKLAND

TEMPORARY ANGEL

A Bantam Book / March 1984
2nd printing . . . July 1989

Bantam Books are published by Bantam Books, a division of
Bantam Doubleday Dell Publishing Group, Inc. Its trade-
mark, consisting of the words "Bantam Books" and the portrayal of a rooster, is Registered in U.S. Patent and Trade-
mark Office and in other countries. Marca Registrada.
Bantam Books, 666 Fifth Avenue, New York, New York 10103.

One

Angie crawled slowly forward across the rocks and fallen earth. When she raised her head more than an inch, she could feel the top of the tunnel brushing against her hair. Every breath she took sounded harsh and loud in the darkness. Fine particles of crushed rock and dirt clogged her nostrils and irritated her mouth.

"God, please," she gasped, "if I'm going to die, let it be in a larger space. Let me do it with dignity . . . not while I'm in this claustrophobic terror."

Suddenly in the midst of the hellish blackness, she heard her father's voice as clearly as if he were there in the tunnel with her. "When the whole boggles you, Angel, forget the whole and tackle it a little piece at a time. Just do what comes next, then carry on from there."

Just do what comes next, she thought, as she moved her hands forward to find enough space to crawl through. The words contained a crazy rhythm that kept her hands and feet moving forward steadily. She banged her head on a low overhang that had escaped her searching hands, but didn't bother to cry out. She simply kept repeating her father's advice over and over mechanically, holding on to it like a talisman.

Hours later—or perhaps minutes, she couldn't be sure—she pushed her hand out to feel the darkness ahead, then drew it back quickly, clapping it over her mouth to hold back a scream of terror. The tunnel was blocked. Where the small opening had been was a solid mass of debris.

"Tackle it a little piece at a time, Angel."

Resting her head on her forearms, she drew in a breath, then began to choke and cough as she inhaled more gritty dust along with the air. She pulled herself up slowly, raised her trembling fingers again to the wall of debris, then steadily began moving her hand to the right over the pieces of rock, farther and farther until she had to shift her body to continue.

The mass of rubble seemed to curve forward and she scrambled frantically around it, ignoring the pain in her hands and knees. On the extreme right she felt the other wall of the tunnel, but between the solid rock of the roof and the debris, she found a space. A tiny space, hardly more than eighteen inches square, but an opening nonetheless.

"No," she whimpered, her breath catching in a dry sob, cold sweat breaking out across her forehead and upper lip. "I can't. It's too much to ask." She beat her fists against the rock; then, feeling blessed anger explode inside her, she shoved herself, hands first, into the narrow fissure.

Grasping the walls with the tips of her fingers, she pulled herself forward inch by inch. Although she could feel the skin being scraped from her bare feet, in a curious way she welcomed the pain. It gave her something besides fear to concentrate on.

Biting back a hysterical laugh, she suddenly realized the space was growing wider. She found she could bend her elbows to get a better grip and began pulling herself forward urgently. With a tremendous burst of adrenaline, she grabbed at the rock wall, clawing it furiously, and then, miraculously, she was free of the tunnel, sliding helplessly down an incline of loose rock and earth. She shielded her head and face with raised arms as she rolled and bounced painfully before coming to an abrupt halt against solid rock.

For long moments she lay motionless, fighting to get her breath back, letting the quakes of reaction subside to teeth-chattering tremors. Then with an aching groan, she hoisted her bruised body into a sitting position and leaned against the rock behind her.

Okay, Jones, she told herself, God answered your prayer and gave you a bigger space to die in. Now what are you going to do? You can't see three inches in front of your face.

She pulled her grimy jacket closer to her body as the cold air in the cave hit the perspiration that covered her body. As she did, she felt something bump against her hip. Reaching into her pocket, she wrapped her fingers around the long, thin object, then with a shaky laugh leaned her head back against the cold rock.

She raised the lighter above her head and spun it to life, flinching at the sudden light as she surveyed her immediate surroundings. The flickering light cast eerie dancing shadows across the fallen rock and settling earth. She lifted her thumb from the lighter and slowly lowered her hand.

What she was viewing had to be the main part of the cave, but it bore no resemblance to the small, damp chamber she had entered earlier with Senator Clements and Art Hammond. Now the fallen rock and earth had filled in the sides of the cave, shrinking it to about half its original size.

"Mac," she muttered weakly, "I'm going to kill you when I get out of here."

She hadn't wanted the dumb story to begin with—a filler that would be hidden away on page ten. And of all the people she could have covered, it had to be Senator Samuel Clements.

"Oh, Lord! Senator Clements!" she gasped suddenly. He was here somewhere. He had to be.

It didn't occur to her until later that she gave no thought to finding the anthropologist who had brought them here to view the newly discovered artifacts. Her thoughts were trained entirely on one man and one man only.

Taking no time to question the desperation that gripped her, Angie began half stumbling, half crawling around the cluttered sides of the cave. She made exasperatingly slow progress, feeling along the edges of the rubble with her hands and feet, afraid to move too slowly for fear the extra minutes would cost him his life, afraid to move too quickly for fear she would miss him.

Gasping frantically for breath, she shifted her position too abruptly and tripped over a large chunk of jagged rock, rolling herself into a ball to protect her face and chest as she fell clumsily forward.

For a moment she lay motionless. "Please, Lord," she whispered hoarsely, her voice shaking, her lips burning from the gritty air. "Please help me this one last time."

Wearily she dragged her arm across her face, wiping away the useless tears on the sleeve of her filthy jacket. Then she stood up and moved back to the heap of stone and earth to begin again. Exhaustion slowed her steps and pulled her body closer to the ground, but she couldn't give up. She couldn't.

Stooping with her arms outstretched to feel her way through the darkness, she moved in the direction of her last position in the rubble, but before she had moved more than a few feet, she stumbled again and fell to her knees, sobbing in frustration as she hit the rough surface and felt fiery shafts of pain shoot up through her body. She placed her hands against the scattered rocks to brace herself as she rose, but suddenly the rocks beneath her hands shifted and she felt something soft underneath.

Pulling the debris aside with frenzied movements, she searched desperately for his head. That it could be Art rather than the senator never occurred to her as she moved her hands across the prone figure. She could feel the muscles of his shoulders and knew he was lying on his face. Pushing at the soft earth that lay around the top part of his body, she found one arm raised above his head, the elbow resting on a large rock.

"There had to have been an air pocket," she rasped. "If he were dead, I'd know—I'd *know*." She dragged at his large body, trying to pull him free of the debris. When she had shifted him away from the rock, she knelt and leaned over him, placing her ear on his chest, but she could hear nothing through the thick shirt he was wearing. Unwilling to trust her trembling fingers with the buttons, she ripped at the shirt, tearing the buttons loose.

Leaning forward, she pressed her ear to his bare, warm chest. Warm! He was still warm—that had to mean something. Shifting her head a few inches, she searched for the elusive heartbeat, then jerked her head up when she heard a faint moan.

Sagging weakly with relief, she allowed herself a few moments to say thank you and to let the tremors that shook her body subside. Then once more she drew out her lighter to make a quick visual examination.

Other than an ugly looking gash on his forehead, she could see nothing obviously wrong. At least he'd stopped bleeding. She returned the lighter to her pocket and began to feel his limbs for broken bones. As she was finishing her examination she felt him move, then his hand touched her hair.

"Jones?"

His voice sounded hoarse, merely a faint reminder of its usual deep resonance. Angie clenched her teeth to keep them from chattering with reaction. When she could trust her voice to remain steady, she whispered, "Yes, Senator. It's me. How do you feel? I didn't find any broken bones."

He gave a short, weak laugh. "I feel like I've been run over by a herd of crazed wildebeest, but I expect I'll make it." Slowly he pulled himself up to a sitting position, cursing sharply under his breath. "How long has it been since the explosion?"

"Explosion?"

"You didn't hear it?" he asked, his voice growing stronger with every word.

"I don't know, I may have," she said, keeping her voice a casual denial of the fear she had felt. "But you can never count on a hysterical fool for information. The first thing I remember clearly is crawling through a space tighter than Aunt Minnie's girdle and going quietly out of my mind. I have a wee touch of claustrophobia," she explained with a short laugh. "I always turn into a drooling lunatic when I'm in an area smaller than Texas Stadium."

She could hear the amusement in his voice as he answered. "Why, Jones, you surprise me. I thought you had printer's ink flowing in your veins. Where's your reporter's cold-blooded objectivity?"

"I lost it the minute I couldn't stand upright," she muttered, then asked, "What kind of explosion?"

"A loud one," he stated grimly. "I don't know anything about explosives, but this one certainly did the trick."

"You mean someone did this deliberately?" she gasped.

"Of course," the senator replied matter-of-factly. "Art doesn't keep anything like that around here.

He's an anthropologist. He has no need for dynamite."

"You seem awfully calm about the whole thing," she said irritably. "Maybe in your line of work you get used to people trying to blow you to bits, but it makes me a teeny bit uncomfortable. The maniac could have at least waited until you were alone."

"Cold-blooded was putting it mildly," he said, chuckling softly. "As hard as this is to believe, I don't think I was the target this time."

"You're not suggesting he was after me?"

"Not you, Art."

"Art!" she gasped in disbelief. "That sweet little man has enemies this deadly? Does he have secret Mafia connections or something?"

"Nothing so exciting I'm afraid," the senator replied drily. "The man I believe to be responsible for this is simply mentally ill. He sent Art a letter warning that if Art moved the bones and stone implements he found here, it would be desecrating the remains of his ancestors. He said he would go to any lengths to stop that."

"He's an Indian? What tribe?" Angie asked, her reporter's nose beginning to twitch.

"No, he's not an Indian, but he believes he is. And even if he were, these artifacts date back to a period before there were established tribes as we know them. I told you he was sick. Maybe now he'll get some help."

"You say Art knows who he—" Angie began, then gasped and began scrambling to her feet. "Art! I forgot all about him. Where is he? He was here with you when I left."

"Hold on. The Senator grasped her arm to pull

her back down. "He went outside to get something before the explosion. You can be sure he's contacted the local officials by now."

"Then all we have to do is wait for them to dig us out," she said, sighing in relief. "I was putting off thinking about how we were going to find the entrance in all this mess. Now I won't have to."

Leaning back against the rocks, she relaxed for the first time in what seemed like years and felt all her muscles begin to throb in unison, as though someone had told them it was all right to hurt now.

"Jones?" he said quietly.

"Yes?"

Thank you for pulling me out."

Angie turned her head away even though he couldn't see her in the darkness. His gratitude made her feel uncomfortable. She didn't want him to be nice to her. Something had happened to her while she was searching for him, something she didn't want to face. She wanted the antagonism between them to continue as it always had.

"I didn't know it was you until I'd already gotten you out," she said shortly. "And it was too much trouble to put the rocks back."

His abrupt laughter echoed loudly in and out of the piles of shattered rock. "You're something else, Jones," he chuckled.

"You just can't figure out what, right?" she said, grinning as their normal insulting banter resumed.

"Jones . . ." He paused for a moment. "Don't you have a first name? I don't think I've ever heard anyone call you anything other than Jones."

"No," she said facetiously. "My mother took one look at my squalling red face and said, 'Oh, shut up, Jones.' Of course I have a first name. It's Angela."

"Angela?"

He sounded surprised, almost shocked, and Angie snorted in indignation. "Well, what did you expect—Scoop?"

"No," he said slowly. "It's just that Angela is so . . . human."

"So what am I?" she asked drily. "A rutabaga?"

"No, of course not," he said, doing a very poor job of hiding his amusement. "I was just a little surprised, that's all. Anyway, thank you for what you did. You probably saved my life."

"How did you know you were buried under that stuff?" she asked gruffly, unwilling to respond to his gratitude. "I thought you were unconscious."

"I came around once, but when I tried to move, something very large and extremely painful hit me on the head and I went out again." He shifted his position, causing a small rock slide beside them. "Where were you when the lights went out?"

"I haven't the vaguest idea," she said. "One minute I was looking at an interesting vein running through the rock wall, then suddenly I was under that interesting vein and there was a mountain of crushed rock and dirt between me and what I thought was the main part of the cave." She shuddered as she remembered the terror. "Considering the state I was in, it's a miracle I didn't start crawling in the wrong direction and end up in a bat roost."

"Yes, we were both lucky to . . ." he began, then paused.

Angie stiffened as she felt him flinch and draw in a sharp breath. "What's wrong? Is it your head?"

"The damn thing's started to bleed again," he said, his voice irritated as though he considered the cut impudent to bother him now.

Stifling a giggle at his tone, she rose to her knees beside him. "Here, let me see." She pulled the lighter from her pocket and flicked it to life, blinking at the sudden light, then held it close to his head to examine the cut that was making a thin trail of blood down the side of his face. "Do you have a handkerchief?"

When he didn't reply immediately, she looked away from the cut and saw he was staring at her.

"Lord, Jones, you look awful," he said, sounding unreasonably surprised as he examined her dirt-encrusted platinum hair and grime-streaked face, then scanned lower to take in her torn, filthy shirt and the once neat slacks that now showed pitifully scraped skin through the jagged holes in the knees.

"I'm a sucker for a sweet-talking man," she cooed, then snatching the handkerchief from his hand as he retrieved it from his hip pocket, she muttered, "Now I wonder why you would think that? In case you haven't noticed, there was a cave-in. I hate to disillusion you, Senator, but even your homespun good looks took a beating in our delightful adventure." She pressed the handkerchief to his forehead with something less than tender loving care.

"Homespun?"

Swearing under her breath as the lighter became uncomfortably hot on her thumb, she released the lever and dropped it back in her pocket before answering. "Sure," she said, her voice casually insulting. "You've got a face that inspires trust—the face of a farmer. But I'm sure you know all about that. I mean, isn't that what you counted on when you went into politics? The curly brown hair that keeps falling across your forehead as though the troubles of the world are constantly weighing you down. The large, rough hands that look like they have just finished plowing a field or birthing a calf. The nose that's just a hair too large and keeps you from being too pretty—thereby capturing the imagination of the women voters, but not offending the men."

She paused, waiting for him to comment. When he remained silent, she continued. "And your name." She gave a short laugh. "Even if it weren't the name of one of the nation's best loved writers, it's such a homey, American kind of name. You automatically trust a man named Sam. Oh, yes, you've got the image down pat, Senator." Sitting down with a sigh, she leaned back and waited for the explosion.

"Whew!" he said softly, his voice rueful. "I take it back. You look lovely."

"Oh, that's typical," she said, her smug grin widening. "I'm honest with you and you interpret it as a feminine tactic and assume I'm trying to get revenge for your honest—but scarcely tactful—remark."

"Jones, I'm tired and my head is throbbing like the devil. I concede your lack of feminine wiles. Now, can we declare a cease-fire for the duration of our stay in this delightful cavern?"

Although his tone was light, she detected a weariness in his voice and immediately her teasing seemed more like careless taunting. Guilt made her uncomfortable, and unreasonably she blamed him for provoking such unusually thoughtless behavior in her.

"I apologize, Senator," she said gruffly. "I wasn't thinking." She paused, biting her lip, then continued grudgingly. "Look, why don't you lay your head in my lap? That will probably stop the throbbing.

"Sam," he said quietly, his voice holding a smile as though he recognized her reluctance.

"I beg your pardon?"

"If I'm going to lay my head in your lap, you can at least call me Sam." With that, he turned to lay his head on her outstretched legs, shifting his body slightly to find a more comfortable space among the rocks.

He moved his head on her lap, in a motion that had it been anyone else she would have described as snuggling, and suddenly Angie regretted her impulsive gesture. The sensations he was causing in her lower body were not what she had expected at all. A slow, tingling warmth radiated outward from where his head lay, concentrating—much to her consternation—in the sensitive area between her thighs.

Good Lord, Jones, she thought in disgust, get thee to a nunnery. The man is injured and simply resting his head, for heaven's sake.

"Very comfortable lap," he murmured suddenly, causing her to jump nervously, and she had to grit her teeth to keep from shifting in discomfort as she felt his warm breath through the thin material of her slacks.

After a few moments of still silence he said in a soft, thoughtful voice, "Angel," then after a pause, "I'll bet when you're asleep, and cleaned up, and when you lay that sharp mind and equally sharp tongue to rest . . . I'll bet you really do look like an angel. An angel with a shaggy silver halo and enormous misty gray eyes." He paused. "You know, Angel, I've always been so busy fielding your questions and sarcastic comments that I never stopped to look at you closely. I don't think I've ever seen you with your mouth closed, but your lips would have to match the rest of you." Yawning noisily, he said, in a voice that sounded as though he were addressing his secretary, "Remind me to check out your lips when we get out of here, Jones."

"Yes sir," she said sarcastically, wishing he could see her so she could finish with a salute. He is the most irritating man, she thought, as she reached down to check on his cut, relieved that the sensations he had caused were subsiding, pushed aside by her irritation.

"You have a remarkably soothing touch, Angel," he murmured, his voice soft and husky as though he were on the brink of sleep. Then in what seemed an unconscious motion, he raised a hand and curled his fingers around her thigh. His warm palm sent an electric vibration that traveled up her leg and through her body and ended in a shiver that shook her delicately.

Suddenly he raised himself to sit beside her and said, his voice rueful, "You're cold. Why didn't you tell me? I can't lay comfortably in your lap while you freeze to death." He chuckled. "You might let the public know how unchivalrous I am."

"But your head," she objected.

"Here," he said, pushing her back against a pile of earth, "if I rest my head on your chest, like this"—Angie clamped her mouth shut to hold back a gasp as he suited his actions to his words—"and wrap my arms around you, like this . . . I think it will solve both problems."

Again he demonstrated his proposal and she found herself wrapped in the warmth of his long, hard body. "This is not necessary," she protested, trying to move away, struggling against the unfamiliar sensations that invaded her body at his touch.

"Cease-fire, Jones—remember?" he reminded her softly, subduing her struggles with an arm around her waist, then when she sighed in resignation and stopped trying to move away, he pressed his body close to hers. "Relax. Tell me about your work. Did you always want to be a reporter?"

"No," she muttered, becoming extremely uncomfortable as she felt the weight of his head on her breast. "When I was five I wanted to be a weight lifter. When I was six I wanted to have my own toenail painting salon. It was only after I gave up those worthy ambitions that I decided to be a reporter."

She relaxed slightly as the memories of her early years brought an accompanying warmth. "When I was in high school my mother wanted me to be what what she called normal. You know—a cheerleader and president of the Future Homemakers of America, but Daddy learned early on that I had to do it my way and he encouraged me to go after what I wanted." She chuckled lazily. "Of course the fact that he was also a reporter might have had something to do with it. What you said about my having printer's ink instead of blood could very well be true. I grew up around the newspaper business and I love it."

"How could your father encourage you to enter a profession that brings you into constant contact with so much suffering? I know there is good news to report as well. But most has to do with the ills that persistently attack the human race. How can you retain your objectivity?"

"That's the pot calling the kettle black," she murmured, her voice growing husky and slow as weariness caught up with her. "How could you choose a profession that daily takes one step forward and two steps back? The frustration would drive me bananas. As for keeping my objectivity, it's not all that difficult. I think I must have something missing in my psychological makeup, because I don't tear myself up over the things I report. At least I don't when it concerns adults," she amended. "It hurts when I see them injured or mistreated by their loved ones or strangers or society, but it's not a consuming horror. It doesn't rip me up like the children do."

She paused. "I know it's not fair to the other reporters I work with, but Mac won't send me out on a story if children are involved. Sometimes I feel guilty about shirking my duty, but since no one has complained, I'll gladly handle the guilt if it means I don't have to see the children. They're so helpless, so . . ."

A shudder ran through her body as haunting memories surfaced and she found herself welcoming the arm around her waist, the warm head on her breast as she fought an old war.

"Don't think about it," he whispered, tightening his hold on her waist. "Put it away for now, Angel."

Closing her eyes she lay still, listening as the sound of his breathing became deep and even, but she didn't want to sleep, didn't want to meet the memories in a nightmare. Long moments later, when she spoke again—over the top of his head to the silent cave—her voice was soft and drowsy as she fought to stay awake.

"I guess I feel some of the same helpless frustration when I think of what we're doing to the earth. I suppose that makes me strange—caring more for the earth than I do for people. But the earth has been here such a long time. It provides everything we need, but we don't own it. We're only allowed to use it while we're here and look what we've done to it. In the short time man has been around we've spread our filth across its entire surface, contaminating the very thing that keeps us alive. It's so incredibly stupid." She sighed, her head drooping. "So stupid."

Feeling herself drift into sleep, she moved her chin away from its resting place on the top of his head and continued, her mind wandering aimlessly. "I suppose earlier, in a less sophisticated time, I would have been a worshiper of trees and rivers and mountains—not a Druid 'cause they were a little overzealous," she added, stifling a yawn. "Now I have to be content with being ecologically conscientious. I guess I'll have to be satisfied with the knowledge that the earth will probably be the only survivor in the not too distant future."

Moving her face against his hair, only vaguely aware of what she was doing, she said sleepily, "I mean, we're not exactly sandhill cranes, are we?"

"Cranes?" His low, soft laughter was muffled against her throat. "Did you say sandhill cranes?"

"Oh Lord," she groaned. "Are you still awake? I thought I put you to sleep ages ago. Ignore everything I've said in the last thirty minutes."

"Oh no," he chuckled and with a couple of movements, Angie was suddenly cradled against his chest. "I want to hear about the cranes."

"You do?" She knew she should object to the move, but his chest with its mat of curling hair was so comfortable, so warm, she couldn't bring herself to move.

"I do."

She sighed in comfort and snuggled closer to his body. "Those cranes have been around for nine million years, much longer than man. They've learned—or maybe, being very smart birds they've always known—that their long, sharp beaks can be lethal weapons. So when they fight for territory—which they do all the time—they don't use their beaks. They jump up and down and screech and throw twigs at each other."

"Are you suggesting we give the army twigs and tell them to jump up and down and screech at the enemy?" he asked, his silent laughter causing her pillow to shake.

"Wouldn't work, huh? I didn't figure it would. I haven't met one single government official that had the intelligence of a crane." She yawned, unaware that he stiffened and tightened his hold when she moved her face against his throat in a sleepy, feline caress. "Maybe I should tell them. I could tell them about UFOs too."

"Tell me instead," he whispered, his voice strangely tight and stiff.

She moved her hand up his chest to rest it on his shoulder beneath his open shirt. "If there really are little green men swooping around the earth, hiding behind clouds and spying on us, they would have to be more advanced in science and technology than we are. As far as our scientists are concerned, travel to another solar system is, if not impossible, totally impractical—that's because of Einstein. But Einstein didn't invalidate Isaac Newton's stuff, he just added to it. Someday someone will come along and add to Einstein's stuff and we'll find we can travel past the speed of light after all." She hesitated as exhaustion caused her to lose her train of thought. "Where was I going with all this. . . . Oh, yeah—people from outer space. If they have managed to survive long enough to advance that far, they must have found the secret to peace that keeps eluding us poor, dumb earthlings and so they are no threat to us.

"Peace on earth," she mumbled sleepily. "Talk about dreaming the impossible dream."

"Not necessarily," he murmured. "If everyone tried to make peace in his own little part of the world, when all the parts connected they would make the peaceful whole. That's where it begins, Angel, in our own little bit of the world."

His voice soothed, drawing her closer until she no longer heard individual words, but was mesmerized by a velvet dream—the dream of perfection in his small corner of the world. He murmured the words against her hair and gently created a new Eden, taking her along with him.

Angie moved restlessly against the sensation that

intruded on her lovely dream world. Still hovering on the edge of sleep, she reached up to brush away whatever was tickling her mouth, but found her hand caught and held.

"Did you just kiss me?" she murmured against his shoulder.

"I was waking Sleeping Beauty."

Pulling away from him to stretch painfully, she muttered, "I think you're in the wrong fairy tale, Senator. And if you think this frog is going to turn into a princess, you're way off base."

He drew her back against him and laughed softly. "Sam . . . remember?"

"Sure, Sam," she said, her tone holding irritation. Memories of what had taken place before she fell asleep were returning and she resented the way he had seduced her into exposing her vulnerability.

"What was that?" she said, jerking her head up as she heard the muffled sound of sliding rocks.

"We're either being rescued," he replied lazily, "or there's a gopher out there I'd prefer not to meet."

Reluctantly she began to laugh. She felt amusement and relief and excitement at the thought of finally being free of their subterranean trap, and unbelievably a touch of regret as she thought of the inevitable loss of the grudging camaraderie they had shared.

Oh, well, she sighed silently. I suppose it's for the best. He was a member of a profession for which she had learned to feel contempt and she knew without a doubt the feeling was mutual. She had been called a vulture on more than one occasion and no doubt Sam—Senator Clements—shared that opinion.

"Angel," he said, interrupting her thoughts. "Before they get here, there's something I want to know."

"Yes?" She raised her head to look up at him even though it was pitch dark, then found her lips captured by his in a soft, exploring kiss and her soft body stiffened in shock.

Raising her hand to push against him, she found suddenly that her fingers had a will of their own as they ran softly across his chest, tentatively testing the warm flesh and hard muscles of his arms and shoulders. Moaning in dismay and unsought pleasure she began to pull her hand away, but he caught it firmly and pushed it back against his chest, next to his heart so she could feel the quickened beat that told her she wasn't experiencing the incredible sensations alone.

As the kiss deepened and his tongue began to penetrate the depths of her mouth in an exploration that sent sensuous tremors through her body, he urged her closer with a firm hand on her buttocks, pressing into her softness. Sliding his hand down her thigh, he lifted it to bring it to rest on his and when she arched convulsively against the evidence of his arousal, he moaned deep in his throat and pressed her back into the soft earth.

"Angel," he whispered feverishly. "Heaven in a dark hell. While you were asleep, I was dreaming—dreaming of this."

He moved his hand inside her jacket, then drew it across her breast to the buttons of her blouse, unfastening them swiftly before she could even acknowledge what he was doing. When his fingers slid inside to cup one full breast, she pulled back abruptly, shaken immeasurably by the sensations his touch provoked.

"You . . . I . . . look," she began to stutter, then suddenly as if out of nowhere, there were voices and somewhere across the small cave, rock began to fall. "They've broken through," she gasped in relief, rising unsteadily to her feet.

Within five minutes they could see beams from the lights of their rescuers and within thirty minutes they were standing beside the cars they had parked earlier in the small field near the cave.

Angie leaned against her ancient Chevy, listening carefully as Art Hammond talked with the local police about the man who had sent the threatening letter. She had lost her notebook and camera—not to mention her shoes—in the cave and didn't want to take a chance on missing any of the details. Occasionally she would glance over to where Sam stood talking to a man in a gray suit. Each time she looked in his direction she would meet his eyes, eyes almost black in the shadows of early evening, and glance away uncomfortably.

At last the police finished their questions and she moved forward hastily to ask a few of her own, then found her progress halted by a firm hand on her arm. She turned to look up questioningly into Sam's eyes.

"Angel," he began quietly. "About what happened in there . . ."

"Look, Senator," she interrupted in a low, urgent whisper, "if you so much as breathe one hint of what happened between us in the cave, I swear I'll spread a rumor that you're a closet transvestite."

Giving a reluctant laugh, he released her arm. "All right, Jones. We'll let it go."

She stared up at him for a moment, then when she saw Art moving toward his pickup, shouted, "Art, wait. I need to talk to you about the fruit-cake who did this. Do you think . . ."

Swearing enthusiastically when her bare feet met unfriendly ground, she hobbled away, her mind busily forming questions and already focused on relaying the information to the night editor. So she missed hearing the softly spoken words that were directed at her retreating back:

"For now, Angel. We'll let it go for now."

Two

Angie slowly entered the smoky little bar that took her from the bright, late afternoon world of cement, tall buildings, and rushing people into a cool, dark grotto filled with the soft murmur of voices and the clink of glasses. She stood just inside the door for a moment, allowing her eyes to adjust.

When she heard her name being called, she pinned a bright smile on her unnaturally pale face before looking up to see Patrick with a beer in one hand, a brunette in the other, and indicating an empty booth with a jerk of his head. Waving to acknowledge the greeting of her large friend, she moved toward the booth in the far corner of the room, absent-mindedly turning aside numerous invitations to join other regulars of the small bar.

Moments after she sat down at the square table, Patrick lowered his large frame onto the vinyl covered seat opposite her with a grunt of disgust as he pushed the table in her direction.

Chuckling, Angie said, "Did anyone ever tell you that you look more like a bouncer than a reporter? Writers are supposed to be thin and aesthetic. With that dumb beard you look remarkably like a Russian weight lifter."

"Is this what I've been waiting half an hour to hear?" he said, raising his empty mug to a passing waitress. "A slanderous attack on my physiognomy?"

"I love it when you talk dirty," she said in a low voice, then gave an impudent grin. "So what has the great Patrick Denby been doing lately, other than trying to seduce innocent maidens." She paused as she was struck by a sudden inspiration. "That's who you remind me of! Robin Hood's faithful Little John—except for the faithful part."

"You really did come here to rip me to pieces, didn't you?" he said, raising one thick, shaggy eyebrow.

"No," she said slowly. "It was all spontaneous honesty. I promise it was unpremeditated, with no malice aforethought."

"If that means you didn't think 'afore' you said it, I believe you. And I forgive you. I know thinking always gives you a headache."

"Okay." She laughed. "You win. There is no possible way to out-insult you. Now tell me what you've been doing. It seems that every time I'm in, you're out."

"I know you think I'm always out covering something of earthshaking import, Ange, but this week

I've been covering the same garbage as everyone else. Today I had the dubious honor of interviewing a man who is suing the city for damaging his garbage cans. And that was the pick of the litter," he said in disgust. "Ed had to go see a woman who lives with seventy-five cats."

He paused to flirt with the cute, young waitress who brought his beer, then turned back to Angie, his eyes sharp, his face suddenly serious. "Okay, kid. What gives? And don't give me that innocent look. Your jolly act doesn't exactly match your eyes. You look like someone snuck up behind you and stole all your blood. Any fool can see something's wrong." He wiggled his eyebrows comically. "And being one of the world's foremost fools, naturally I spotted it right away. So come on, spill your guts for Uncle Patrick."

"You are a fool." Angie laughed shakily, avoiding his eyes as she reached in her purse for a cigarette. But her hand trembled so violently she gave up and leaned her head back against the seat wearily. "I had lunch with Mac today," she said quietly.

"And?"

"Oh, it started off like it always does. With me asking for a story with some real meat to it and him putting me off." She raised her head sharply as she remembered the conversation. "Do you know what he had the nerve to say when I asked him for a real story? He said, 'Didn't I give you that great bomb story last week? Nobody else on the staff got a bomb story,' " she mimicked.

She eyed Pat evilly when he burst out laughing. "He knows good and well the only reason I got to cover that story was because I was under the bomb with Senator Clements when it went off. He didn't send me to cover a bomb story or even to cover the discovery of the artifacts, but to cover a grinning politician viewing the artifacts! The whole thing stinks."

"Let me guess what he said when you told him that," Pat said. "He said, 'You point out the man who told you life was fair, Jones, and I'll call him a liar to his face.'" Pat rolled his eyes. "Mac needs a new scriptwriter. He only knows four sentences and they're wearing pretty thin." He reached out to tip up her chin. "And is that what made you look like an advertisement for death?"

"No," she whispered. "I wouldn't let it go this time. I wanted some straight answers." She heaved a deep sigh. "I've been a reporter for ten years now—eight with the *Monitor* and almost two with the *Star.* I've covered everything from society news to bank robberies. I simply wanted to know why he keeps shoving these damnfool stories off on me."

"And did he tell you?" Pat's voice held something dangerously close to pity, as though he already knew the answer.

"He said my writing is excellent. My facts always hold up. I can smell a story a mile away, but"—she swallowed hard, tightening her lips to keep them from trembling—"I just don't have the objectivity you need to be a reporter." She met Patrick's eyes. "He knows what he's talking about, doesn't he?"

Patrick nodded slowly. "I'm sorry, babe."

"You saw it too?" she asked in defeat.

"It was that first story you covered after you came here. I saw your eyes after you interviewed that poor woman. Ange, he couldn't send you out on anything like that again; it would have broken you sooner or later. It was more than just feeling horror because a child was dead. It was eating away at you. Your eyes had a glazed look for months after that."

He picked up her hand and gave it a comforting squeeze. "You try so hard to be tough, but you can't hide that kind of pain." He paused. "So what did Mac suggest?"

She leaned her head forward in dejection, the spiky, feathered tips of her silver-blond hair curling around her fingers as she rested her delicate pointed chin on the palm of her hand. "He said he would think about letting me cover the police station." She snorted in disgust. "The police station! Drunks, drug addicts, and prostitutes. And if a real story came in, he would send someone else to cover it. No thanks."

"Listen, Ange, there's something I want to talk to you about," Pat began, leaning closer, his face intent. But before he could finish, they were interrupted by another member of the *Star* staff.

"Hey, Angie," Charlie Duncan, a thin, stooped man, called. "What was it like to be trapped for hours with the honorable senator from our Lone Star State? You didn't say a word about it in your article."

Angie's views on politicians were well known and she knew he and Pat were waiting for her to begin verbally abusing the senator. "Sure I did," she said, shifting uncomfortably. "I quoted Senator Clements several times in the article."

"I didn't ask what it was like for him. I asked what it was like for you. You could have built that into a great story if you had written it from an eyewitness point of view."

"Well, I didn't, did I," she said irritably. "So I guess I'll just have to be satisfied with a good story instead of a great one."

When someone caught Charlie's attention and he wandered away, Pat trained narrowed blue eyes in her direction. "What's the matter, Ange? Did the Senator get a little too friendly? You want me to go punch him? Or better yet, we could expose him publicly as a dirty old man. . . ."

"Patrick!" she gasped, then saw the gleam of white teeth through his unkempt mustache. "You idiot. I thought you were serious. Nothing happened in the cave. And even if it had, I can handle my own affairs. Business affairs," she amended when she saw his gleefully raised eyebrows.

"Tsk, tsk. We're certainly touchy, aren't we. If I didn't know better I would say the good senator charmed you like he has the rest of the country. Now you've got me curious."

"Patrick, don't be curious," she said warily. "It can only lead to trouble. And most likely trouble for me. Now, please, can we change the subject?"

"Sure. I'm easy," he said, grinning, then reached across the table to punch her softly when she nodded in agreement. "So. Did you hear Senator Clements' speech yesterday?"

"Pat!" she said in exasperation. "I said I didn't want to talk about him. You know how I feel about politicians." She paused, remembering the softly spoken words that had mesmerized her in the cave. "Actually I think Senator Clements might be the exception," she murmured, her eyes turning soft, misty gray. "Although any public office has the potential to corrupt, he seems like a basically honest man who all too frequently finds that his hands are tied."

As what she was saying slowly sank in, Angie's mouth dropped open in surprise. Now when on earth had she come up with those astounding conclusions? She had always been biased against politicians in general and Senator Clements in particular. A glance at Pat told her the astonishing about-face had affected him in the same way. Was she really so weak-minded that one kiss from an attractive man could change convictions she had thought were deeply imbedded in her character?

Grabbing her purse, she mumbled an excuse to the still frozen Patrick and headed for the ladies' room to compose her scattered wits.

In the dingy little bathroom, Angie looked into the mirror above the bare sink, taking a comb from her purse to run it irritably through the fine blond hair that framed her face with its feathery tips and barely brushed her shoulders in a ragged pageboy.

"A shaggy silver halo," he had called it. She shook her head in confusion at the way her thoughts kept veering toward Sam Clements. What was it about that man? Why did he keep popping into her head, mental images of him insidiously creeping up on her when she least expected them?

It was an extremely uncomfortable situation, to say the least. All week long she had found him intruding into her thoughts, interfering with her life, even her work. When she had gone down to the morgue to go through the files for background material on a building due for destruction, she had suddenly found herself researching instead the background of one Samuel Clements, lawmaker par excellency.

All the facts were known to her. She had been over them dozens of times since she had first encountered the senator three years earlier while she had still been employed by her hometown newspaper. But she went over the material as though seeing it for the first time.

Thirty-five years ago he had been born to upper-middle-class parents in a suburb of Austin. It was only after he had studied law at Harvard and Northwestern universities that he had caught the public eye, serving as special adviser to the Agriculture Stabilization and Conservation Service at the tender age of twenty-seven. From there it had been a short step to the Senate and his role as the ordinary man's voice in government.

But for all her digging, Angie had uncovered no more than a token amount of information concerning his personal life. He was seen from time to time with various women—all of them beautiful, all of them discreetly mannered—but none of them, apparently, permanent.

In a flash of honesty, Angie admitted that the antagonism she felt toward him was not only because he held public office. All her investigations pointed to the fact that he was, on the surface, an honest man trying to do a difficult job. No, part of the animosity stemmed from something more personal. An intuitive feeling that when those brown eyes lingered on her, he was seeing more than was on the surface, right to the secret parts that no one before him had seen. It was a disquieting sensation, exposing a vulnerability she preferred to hide.

Walking back to the table, she suddenly remembered her lunch with Mac and was stunned that anything could have taken her mind off it. "The man's a warlock," she muttered incredulously.

As she glanced up, her mouth dropped open in surprise. Sitting across the table from Pat was the most astonishing man she had ever seen. He looked like a leftover flower child, his iron-gray hair held in place by a grubby headband, his clothes as though they had not seen a washing machine since the turbulent era that had given birth to his hairstyle. As she drew nearer the man gave her a furtive look, then stood quickly and faded into a group of people standing near the bar.

"Who or what was that?" she asked in disbelief as she slid into the booth.

"Didn't you recognize him?" Patrick asked with a grin. "That was Michael Faraday."

"Faraday?" Her forehead creased in thought as she tried to place the strange man, then her eyes widened incredulously. "You mean the activist from the sixties? But he was an old man even then. He must be ancient now."

"No one knows how old. They can't make him stand still long enough to carbon date him."

"So what was he doing here? And more to the point, what was he doing with you? Since when have you been interested in over-the-hill hippies?"

"That's what I was trying to tell you about earlier," he said enthusiastically. "Why I asked you to meet me here tonight. I mean, I'm always interested in trying to make it with you, but that's only reason number two tonight."

"And reason number one?"

"How does this hit you—'Portrait of an Anachronism.' Or maybe 'Echoes of Anger.' "

"As a feature story or a series of articles?" she asked casually, even though the gears in her brain were whirring furiously at the possibilities unraveling before her.

"Neither," he said, his voice lowered to a whisper. "A book."

She felt her pulses leap as his quietly spoken words reached her ears. "Do you have enough material? That era has been pretty well worked out. You would have to come up with a fresh, new angle. . . . No, more than that—it would have to be damned sensational to get a publisher interested."

"I think his view of present-day activists alone is worth the time, but there's more." He spoke calmly, his tone giving no clue to his next startling words. "He just happens to be knee deep in the underground activity that's going on right now."

"But there's no heavy activity going on now. At least nothing organized."

"That's what you think," Patrick said smugly. "I've only scratched the surface of it, Ange, but it's big. It's not a visible movement. It's all hidden and carefully planned out, unlike the random violence of the sixties. And it's more widespread than the Weathermen ever thought of being."

"You have proof?"

"I can get it. And this book will blow the lid wide open. Our fortunes will be made, kid."

"Just where do I come in?" she asked, eyeing him suspiciously.

"It will be a collaboration," he hedged. "Denby and Jones."

"Why?" she persisted, afraid to let the excitement take hold until she knew what his angle was. Patrick always had an angle.

"It's exactly what you need," he said, avoiding her eyes. "When Mac told you he was going to keep giving you poached egg stories, what did you decide to do?"

"I don't know. I guess I was considering freelancing for a while."

"Right. So you're going to be leaving the paper anyway. This would give you something to work on while you get things straight." He paused, smiling at her benevolently. "You've got the money your grandmother left you, so money's no problem. It's perfect."

"And you concocted this little scheme on the spur of the moment, simply to help me over a rough spot in my life," she said skeptically. "Come on, Pat, the truth."

"I was afraid you wouldn't buy that." He sighed with regret. "The truth is I need your help. I hate to admit it, but there are some things about this character I simply can't grasp. You know I'm single-minded about some things. Some people might even say hard-headed." He glared at her when her lips formed an O of disbelief. "Okay, I admit it. The thing is Ange, I can't get into his head and feel what it was all about back then. I mean I was just a kid when all this was happening. I can't relate to it. But you can. You have a kind of timeless empathy. I've seen you do it. When you interviewed that old lady who ran a bawdy house during Prohibition, your story made me feel I was an eyewitness to the whole thing and understood the way people were thinking back then." He reached across the table to grasp her hand urgently. "So how about it? Will you help me?"

"My name on the front cover?" she asked nonchalantly, lighting a cigarette as her heart began to pound with excitement. "No polite thank-you in the acknowledgements, but my name equal in size to yours on the front cover. Right?"

"You're a hard-hearted woman, Angela Jones," he said mournfully. "But you've got yourself a deal."

Laughing in relief and elation, she asked, "How do you know he'll talk to me? He looked awfully timid."

"Are you kidding? The one thing he loves more than giving a rousing diatribe against the government is a luscious blonde." Patrick gave her a wicked leer. "So don't worry about that."

"I'd better tell you right now, Pat," she informed him drily. "There are some things I won't do, even for a story. Sleeping with that spooky old man is one of them."

He gave a snort of mock contempt. "And you call yourself a reporter." Chuckling, he added, "That won't be necessary. To tell you the truth, I don't think he could even if you were willing. Of course, if you would consider a spooky *young* man, I very definitely can."

Ignoring his half-hearted attempts to seduce her, she began to throw eager questions at her burly friend, but before she could extract any useful information from him, they were joined by a group of their friends. And when it looked as though the entire group was going to follow them to a café for dinner, Angie begged off, promising to get in touch with Patrick the following day so he could outline his strategy.

This was the opportunity she needed, she thought eagerly as she let herself into her apartment half an hour later. If she used it wisely, it could mean a complete turnaround for her career. It could be the stepping stone she needed to build herself a reputation.

The past ten years had gone so quickly. She had intended to remain with her first employers for only a short time. Just long enough to get started in the right direction. But it was always next year that she would leave to follow her dream, until suddenly she woke up and saw the dream slipping away.

So she had packed her bags and headed for the big city and a busy, metropolitan newspaper, away from the small town that had offered such limited scope for her natural capabilities—only to find herself trapped in the same situation.

But that's all going to change now, she promised herself, laughing with pure pleasure at the thought. Nothing can stop me now.

"Except maybe hunger," she added aloud as her stomach began to complain about her neglect. She stripped off her clothes, pulled on a loose cotton robe, and slid the front zipper up as she walked into the kitchen for crackers and cheese.

"And kosher dill pickles," she promised her stomach, pouring a large glass of milk.

When the doorbell rang minutes later, she hurriedly stuffed a cracker in her mouth and carried the glass with her to the door, assuming it was her next-door neighbor who never seemed to make it through dinner without borrowing something.

"Diane . . ." she began, then raised her eyes from the spot where her petite friend's face should have been to the spot a good twelve inches higher where she found the face of Senator Samuel Clements.

Three

Angie began to cough furiously when the deep
breath she had drawn in at the sight of him standing in her doorway caused pieces of cracker to enter
her windpipe. With watering gray eyes she glanced
up at the man who had caused her dilemma and
was now enthusiastically pounding her on the back.

"That's enough," she gasped weakly, then her
brow creased as curiosity overcame her indignation. "What are you doing here, Senator?"

Smiling slightly at the bluntness of her question,
he said, "May I come in?"

She stood aside and waved him into the large,
old-fashioned living room. "Certainly," she said
airily. "Come in and sit down—you can even prop
your feet up if you like. Then tell me what you're
doing on my doorstep at this time of the night—or
at all for that matter."

Laughing softly, he sat down on the long couch, keeping his eyes trained on her as she sat on the edge of the chair opposite him and took a sip of milk to clear her raspy throat.

"You've got a biting sense of humor, Jones. I like that."

She raised one delicately arched eyebrow in surprise. "Oh, really? And when did you come to that startling conclusion?"

"In the cave. As a matter of fact, I came to quite a few startling conclusions in the cave."

"Oh?" she murmured, keeping her voice uninterested as her heart began to beat in a crazy, thumping rhythm.

"Yes," he confirmed, leaning back to stretch out his long legs casually. "Don't you want to know what they were?"

"Not particularly," she lied, smiling sweetly. "But I have a feeling I'm going to find out anyway."

"Maybe deadly would be a better description than biting," he chuckled, then looked around the room in curiosity. "This is a very honest room, Jones."

She glanced around the large, open room, seeing it not as home, but as if she were walking into it for the first time. It was a room that welcomed, that invited one to relax. While it didn't intimidate with perfection, neither did it irritate with unnecessary clutter. The odd pieces of furniture she had picked up over the years shared the room comfortably like a group of old friends sitting around a checkerboard. And Sam Clements looked as though he belonged as surely as the high-backed couch on which he sat.

This last disturbing thought caused her to shift

uncomfortably. Irritated at his ability to fit into surroundings that were exclusively hers, she repeated, "Why are you here, Senator?"

Drawing up his legs, he leaned forward to rest his forearms on his knees and eyed her intently. "If I ask you a question, will you answer it honestly?"

"Of course." She answered without hesitation. "*Reporters* are not known for giving evasive answers."

"Good." He leaned back to his former relaxed position, ignoring her implied insult. "What happened between us just before we left the cave—does that happen to you often?" When she snapped her head up in surprise, he added, "I don't mean the physical act. I mean the depth, the intensity of the whole thing. You must have felt it; it was too powerful to have been one-sided."

Angie stared in blank astonishment, her features frozen. His words didn't match his tone. He sounded as though he were discussing a budget proposal rather than an intimate incident between two people. At a loss as to how she should respond, she remained silent for a moment, then remembering her promise of honesty, cleared her throat nervously. "I'll admit what happened between us was not an ordinary occurrence, but I've come to the conclusion that the intensity was due to the unusual circumstances."

"Then you have thought about it," he said, pouncing on her words with puzzling speed.

"Don't be stupid." She placed her glass on the end table and stood in agitation. "Of course I've thought about it." She gave a short laugh. "It's not every day a cave falls in on top of me."

"And you think the depth of feeling was due entirely to the harrowing nature of our shared experience?"

"Counsel is badgering the witness," she muttered peevishly, then as he began to laugh, "Yes, that's exactly what I think. Now can we drop it?"

"Not yet. Don't you think we should test your theory—just in case?"

She stood before him, staring warily at his face. "Just in case?"

"We wouldn't want to reach the wrong conclusion, now would we?"

His voice had grown soft, mesmerizing her with the warm, velvet quality that had enthralled her in the cave. Swallowing nervously, she glanced away from the light growing in his eyes. "What are you proposing?"

Although her head was turned away from him, she could feel his eyes on her as he spoke. "I think we should reenact the event in question—now—in a more normal atmosphere." When she made no comment, he added softly, "You aren't afraid of being proven wrong, are you?"

"No . . ." Her voice was thin and breathless, holding only a hint of its normal strength. She cleared her throat and began again in a firmer voice. "No, of course not." She turned to look at him. "I think it's totally unnecessary, but if it will satisfy you—" When she saw his lips twitch in amusement, she amended her words. "Make you go away, that is, I'll do it."

His mouth lifted at the corners, deepening the grooves along the side of his face, showing even, white teeth. He held her eyes and gently patted the couch beside him.

Her immediate reaction was to back down, to put him off with excuses, but the challenging gleam she saw in his dark eyes had her stiffening her back and moving to sit beside him. Closing her eyes, she turned her head and offered him stiff, belligerent lips.

Long, awkward moments passed before she opened her eyes to give him an exasperated look, only to find he had moved silently closer, his lips a fraction of an inch away from hers.

"With your eyes open, Angel," he murmured huskily, his breath causing the sensitive flesh of her lips to tingle crazily. "It was dark in the cave. This time I want you to see who you're kissing."

With the last word he closed the small gap between them and she felt his firm, full lips brush gently across hers. Her eyelids drooped momentarily as a lethargic warmth invaded her body, then opened wide when he cupped her neck with his large hand to hold her securely.

In the beginning his immobile mouth merely covered hers, giving her time to adjust to the feel of him, then slowly it began to move against hers, gently sucking at her lower lip, coaxing her to give him access to the sensitive depths.

The deep brown eyes that held her gray ones captive sapped her will, demanding that she part her lips to receive the tongue that probed the corners of her mouth and teased the tender inner flesh of her full lower lip.

At her first hesitant sign of surrender—a slight trembling movement—the tenor of his seduction changed with breathtaking swiftness. No power on earth could have held her eyes open when he moved his hand to the small of her back, pulling her close as his tongue entered triumphantly to explore the warm, moist interior with increasingly urgent strokes.

Lifting her hand to grasp the taut muscles of his neck, she held onto the kiss with an intensity that was foreign to her. She matched the movement of his tongue with eager strokes of her own, moaning involuntarily when he caught it and sucked at it gently.

As though the sound of her pleasure had signaled the end of the match, his movements slowed and he eased her back to earth gradually, ending the encounter with a series of short, soft kisses before he withdrew completely and turned to lean his head back against the couch, his eyes drifting shut.

"Definitely not the cave-in," he murmured, his voice sounding rough and strained.

Shifting her eyes away from his reclining figure to look straight ahead, Angie swallowed nervously, coughed to clear her throat, then stared with intense concentration at a small print on the opposite wall. "No," she whispered. Her voice sounded strangely hoarse and loud in the silent room. She shook her head to clear away the sensual mist and drew in a deep, bracing breath, making a visible effort to pull herself together. "But just exactly what does that prove? What do you suggest we do now—appoint a committee to investigate the possible alternatives, or simply vote on a course of action?"

She felt him move beside her, pulling his large frame upright, then his hand rested gently on her cheek and he moved her face toward him. "I propose we carry the attraction through to its logical conclusion," he said quietly.

She stared at him blankly, responding to his touch and the sound of his voice rather than his words, then as his meaning penetrated her misty spell, she pulled her head away and rose abruptly. "You would," she muttered irritably, pausing in her stride to pick up a cigarette from the end table. She lit it with hands that—much to her annoyance—trembled slightly, and went to stand in front of the window, where she looked out into the night with unseeing eyes.

"In the first place," she said, speaking slowly and firmly, "I don't think the conclusion you're referring to is necessarily logical and in the second place"—she glanced at him over her shoulder— "if I had the time or inclination to enter into a temporary affair—which I haven't—it would definitely not be with a politician."

His lips twisted in a crooked smile that made him look almost vulnerable. "It took me a while to accept the fact that I was this deeply attracted to a reporter," he said drily. "But I had to. It didn't go away just because it was inconvenient." He paused. "What have you got against politicians anyway?"

"Professionally or personally?"

"I think you've made your professional views crystal clear over the last three years." He rose and stood close behind her. "But there's more to it than that. Why are you personally antagonistic toward people who hold public office?"

She drew deeply on the cigarette, exhaling the smoke slowly as she felt his nearness and fought her need to lean against him. "Politicians are a special breed, Senator," she said, her voice sounding disinterested. "I don't have to tell you that."

"Sam," he commanded quietly.

"Sam," she repeated in exasperation. She moved away from the window to break the sensual threads that tried to bind her to him. "I was involved with a junior league public servant once—for a very short time, thank God. The break-up of our dubious association didn't exactly leave me devastated, but the lesson I learned stuck and everything I've seen since has reinforced my original impression. Nothing comes before politics and personal relationships don't even merit second place. The ego of the future president or governor or whatever has to be constantly fed. Companions are chosen with the public in mind rather than the presence of any genuine feeling. And heaven help you if you don't fit the mold."

"You're basing your opinion on one man," he said calmly. "Not everyone in politics is like that."

She swung around to face him, feeling in some way that she was fighting for her life. "Bullsh—"

"Don't swear," he interrupted, casually removing the cigarette from her fingers to stub it out in an ashtray.

"You see!" she shouted, anger building visibly in her eyes. "You're already trying to change me. And we're not even sleeping together."

"Yet," he added with a soft laugh that fueled her fury. "And I'm not trying to change you. You smoke and swear to make yourself look hard." His voice dropped to a husky whisper. "But you're not hard, are you, Angel? You're soft and warm and sweet."

"No!" Her shout echoed loudly as she fought the spell his deep voice wove around her. "I'm not. I'm not an angel either. And I won't pretend to be, even temporarily." She drew in a deep, harsh breath. "I've been through it before, Sen—Sam. It starts with the little things. Then gradually it creeps into every area of your life until one day you look up and find yourself wearing shirts with alligators on the pockets and watching every move you make in public, smiling an idiot smile at everything that moves in case it can vote. You wake up to find your soul has been sucked away and in its place is a public image."

He leaned against the wall, watching her with interest as she talked herself into a fine state of indignation, his face never losing its crooked smile.

Staring at his bemused features belligerently, she continued. "And that's only if you're lucky. If you don't measure up—even with all the changes—then you get the doubtful honor of creeping around to hide the fact that a public servant spends his non-public hours with you."

Glancing at him disdainfully, she said, "Thanks, but no thanks."

He reached out and with his index finger outlined her full lips. "Relax," he said softly. "I don't like to see you purse your lips like that. You have a very sexy mouth, full and soft and made to give pleasure—made to give *me* pleasure."

"Haven't you been listening to me?" she asked in exasperation.

His hands moved to her hips and he drew her closer. "I listened long enough to find out that what you were saying had nothing to do with us."

Angie groaned in frustration. "There is no us!"

"No?" he whispered as he molded her lower body to his, moving her hips gently from side to side, bringing her to a full awareness of his arousal, stroking her most vulnerable part with his hardened masculinity. "That's odd," he murmured huskily as her eyes drifted shut and a look that resembled pain crossed her features. "It definitely feels like there's an us."

The hypnotic effect of his voice, the erotic movement of her body against his, drained Angie of all anger, sapped her will and her strength. She made no move to halt the fingers that slowly slid the zipper down to her waist.

"You're working on a false premise, Angel." His voice stroked her senses, soothing away her last bit of resistance. "You're assuming I'm like some brainless twit you once knew. I wouldn't compare you with anyone else because you are you—not a carbon copy, not a plastic duplication."

His large hands slid inside her robe to rest on her ribs. "All I'm asking is that you give me the same consideration."

He moved his hands up her sides under her arms to rest on the swelling edges of her breasts, parting the robe slowly, and she heard his swift intake of breath as though from a great distance. His voice when he finally spoke was rough with emotion.

"As for trying to change you to suit some ephemeral mold, the thought is ridiculous. All I want to do is show you that the wall you've built around yourself—the face you show the rest of the world—is not necessary with me."

His thumbs began an erotic circular massage of the hardened tips of her burgeoning breasts and her head sagged back weakly as the spiraling sensations shook her body, her breath coming in harsh gasps.

"You're not tough, Angel. I know. You've let me feel your warmth, I've been welcomed by your softness."

Cupping her full breasts, he rolled the taut, sensitive nipples between his forefingers and thumbs, tugging at them gently to send shafts of sensual pleasure streaking on a sizzling course to her lower limbs, compelling her to arch against him to ease the throbbing ache.

"Why are you fighting it? I can feel the want in you." His hoarse whisper caressed her ear, his heated breath sent her own temperature soaring. "Be my angel tonight. Let me come into your warmth. I want to feel it surround me, pull away the ache in me."

The tongue that sought the crevices of her ear, the fingers that slipped across her warm, bare hip to stray unbearably close to the curl-covered mound of flesh that held the center of her aching need, the erotic words his raspy voice murmured, enticed her on to discover his secret world—a world of unknown, unmeasurable pleasure.

She found herself parting her lips to say the words that would bring his hand down to claim the heated spot between her thighs, grasping his shoulders urgently to secure the promised ecstasy. But then as though a spotlight had been focused on their entwined bodies, the knowledge of what was happening hit her forcefully and she drew back sharply, her dazed eyes widening with shock.

Turning away swiftly, she pulled up the zipper on her robe with trembling fingers and leaned against the wall weakly, willing her heart to stop shaking, her heart to stop pounding in her chest. "I think I'll put my money on you in the next presidential election," she said, giving an unsteady laugh. "You certainly have a way with . . . words."

Glancing over her shoulder, she found he was still standing where she had left him. His eyes were closed, his hands pushed deep in the pockets of his brown slacks, his chest expanding beneath the cream V-necked sweater as he drew in a deep breath.

Opening his eyes slowly, he stared at her and smiled wryly. "Believe it or not, the presidency is the last thing on my mind right now."

It was incredible the way his voice, his taut, muscular body pulled at her senses. Avoiding his eyes uneasily, she said, "I think it's time you left, Sam."

"This can't be the end of it, Angel," he said quietly. "You felt what was happening between us. It's not something you can ignore." When she remained silent, he continued. "Suppose you're wrong about the way you would be affected by an affair between us? Isn't what we just shared worth the time to find out?"

Angie clenched her fists as his voice began to wrap its magic softness around her. "What is it?" she whispered desperately. "What is it that you want from me?"

"Nothing that would threaten or compromise you." His voice came from directly behind her and she felt his hand on her shoulder, turning her around to face him. "Have dinner with me tomorrow night. Find out for yourself if I'm a machine that would suck up your soul."

His nearness swamped her. She had to fight to

keep from brushing the lock of hair off his forehead, to keep from pressing herself against him and crying, "Uncle!"

In her desperate fight against her traitorous body, she would have promised him almost anything to regain control of her senses. "Yes," she whispered through stiff lips. "Dinner tomorrow."

He framed her face with his hands and brushed his mouth across hers, sipping gently at her lips as though reluctant to leave their warmth, then pulled back with a sigh.

"You won't regret it, Angel," he whispered before turning to walk to the door.

Slumping weakly into a chair, she watched him leave, muttering, "Would you like to make a bet on that, Senator?" to the closed door, as regret and doubt took hold and shook her weakened body.

Four

Angie stared at her wide-open gray eyes in the mahogany-framed mirror, adding a last touch of mascara to disclose the true length of their pale fringe. Then laying the tube aside, she lowered her gaze to the gentle smile that curled her peach-tinted lips.

"Jones!" she scolded. "You're smiling. The man coerced you into going out with him and you stand there grinning like you have two pounds of pineapple yogurt between your ears."

Pulling her lips into a frown, she leaned close to the image in the mirror. "Coercion is not a pretty business. For heaven's sake, serious up."

She gave her grim face a satisfied nod and turned away, unaware that her mouth turned up irresistibly as she did. Glancing at the old-fashioned round alarm clock on her bedside table she saw more incriminating evidence. Sam was not due to arrive for another half hour. And except for her dress and shoes, she was ready to go. She was never ready this early. It was almost as though she were anxious to see him.

That's ridiculous, she assured herself silently. I simply want to get it over with. He's the enemy. A died-in-the-wool, honest to God political machine. He's—he's a man who makes your knees go guacamole, she admitted wryly. And if that's a machine, you'd better buy stock in the company that manufactures it because they'll sell a million.

Flopping down on the bed in confusion, she lowered her gaze to her nylon-covered toes. What was happening to her? One minute she was living her life almost by rote, then overnight everything had changed. Suddenly the path she had been blithely following had veered sharply, taking her unprepared into unknown territory. She was twenty-seven years old. Her goals should have been well established by now. She had mistakenly thought they were. Now she found she was unfit for the career at which she had worked so hard and was about to take on something completely out of her scope.

Mac had been sympathetic—almost relieved—when she had given notice and told him of her plans. Although he had asked her to contribute articles on a free-lance basis, his reaction had been another blow to her self-esteem. The challenge of starting over was exciting; the project Pat had mapped out over the phone this afternoon was intriguing; but the bad taste of failure lingered in her mind, tainting the excitement and intrigue.

And through all the indecision, through all the emotions, good and bad, a brown-eyed senator lurked on the fringes of her mind, at times overshadowing even her all-important career. His growing importance in her thoughts bothered her. The way she had begun to see him, not as a news story, not as a politician, but as a man, bothered her. In fact, everything about the dratted man bothered her.

Seeing him tonight was a mistake. She could feel it in her bones. The attraction between them was much too strong. It could only lead to trouble.

She had managed very well without the physical side of life until now. Why was she faced with this stunning attraction at this point in her life? After the laughable episode that had taken place when she was a very unworldly eighteen, she had shoved all that into the background, preferring to concentrate on her career. And until the intrusion of a certain senator, she had been perfectly content with the status quo. Now it seemed that all those emotionally barren years were catching up with her. As though her body had been on hold until a man with a crooked smile had pushed the right button.

She stood in exasperation and walked to the closet to draw out the pale green silk dress she had chosen for the evening. "It probably doesn't have anything to do with Sam," she muttered. "It's probably a simple case of late-developing puberty—or premature menopause. Hot flashes and palpitations!" she snorted in derision, thinking wryly as she stepped into her dress that a hormone shot would have been a much safer course of action.

She would give it tonight. She would keep her eyes and ears open and see exactly what kind of man he was. Then she would tell him to get lost because she had no doubt that her observations would confirm her admittedly biased original opinion: a politician is a politician is a politician.

As she was slipping into the green evening sandals, the doorbell rang and she took a last, quick look in the mirror. The modest V of her long-sleeved sheath showed just a hint of the creamy swell of her breasts, the silk hugged her figure with a subdued sensuality of which she was totally unaware. Her platinum hair framed her face with soft, silver feathers and the addition of mascara had enlarged her eyes until they almost seemed to fill her face.

Giving the figure in the mirror a casual once-over, she shrugged. "I won't cause any riots in the street," she murmured in unconcern. "But I won't disgrace myself either." Turning away, she headed for the living room when the doorbell rang again.

As she reached the door she inhaled deeply, then pulled it open. The flip words that had been forming died in her throat when she saw him standing in the hall. She overlooked the beautifully tailored brown suit as her eyes settled with rapt attention on his face. A lock of curly hair fell across his forehead and his tanned features were creased by a gentle smile.

"Sam," she said, and much to her chagrin, her voice came out soft and breathy, a bemused smile lifting the corners of her mouth.

His smile deepened, his eyes sparkling with surprise and something that was beyond her comprehension. "Why, Angel," he said. "You almost sound pleased to see me."

Angie glanced away in irritation. *Good Lord, Jones, get that nauseating grin off your face.*

Stiffening in determination, she met his eyes squarely. "That wasn't pleasure," she said, lying without conscience. "That was relief. I thought you were a magazine salesman."

He laughed softly, tilting her chin with his index finger to give her a fleeting kiss. "Hello, Angel," he murmured, then when she backed away and raised a hand to rub her mouth, he caught it in his. "No, don't wipe it off. You'll smear your lipstick."

"Well, *you* had better wipe it off," she muttered drily. "The color clashes with your tie." As he pulled out his handkerchief to remove the smear of lipstick, she glanced away skittishly and asked, "Would you like a drink before we leave?"

"No, thank you."

She heard the smile in his voice and gritted her teeth in irritation. Inhaling slowly, she thought angrily how everything about this man irritated her.

Everything, Jones? came the insidious thought.

She shook her head, forcing the question out of her mind and walked to the sofa to pick up the cashmere shawl the cool spring evening made necessary.

As she walked beside him to his car, listening to his lazy comments on the weather, she realized she was going to make her evening more uncomfortable if she gave in to the tight knot of tension that lay like a stone in the center of her stomach.

Relax, she advised silently. It's only for one night. Enjoy it.

When they were both settled in his large, comfortable car, she glanced toward him and smiled slowly, then watched as lines of puzzlement creased his forehead. She decided smugly that her change of attitude was the right move if only because it gave her such pleasure to see him thrown off balance.

He stared at her intently for a moment, then turned away to start the car. "Angel," he said slowly, "you're not allergic to Chicken à la King, are you?"

She chuckled irresistibly at his hesitant tone. "I know I'm going to hate myself for this, but why do you ask?"

"I wanted this to be a quiet evening for the two of us. A chance for us to get to know each other," he murmured, then sighed in resignation. "Do you know Charles Apperly?"

"The president of the Chamber of Commerce?"

Nodding, he said, "He's a personal friend. I had forgotten about the awards dinner tonight until he called to remind me. I'm afraid there was no way I could get out of it."

After a brief, inexplicable moment of disappointment, she realized this was the opportunity she was looking for. She could observe him with the public and see for herself if he hedged issues and tried to please everyone. Every person attending the dinner was a potential vote and they all had to be wooed—at the expense of his personal integrity.

When they walked into the banquet room of the large, downtown hotel and Angie passed a jaundiced eye over the white-draped tables that were

arranged in an open-ended rectangle, she was ready
to mentally record his downfall.

Contrary to Sam's warning the food had been
excellent, prime rib providing a welcome substi-
tute for the chicken he had predicted. Angie had
contributed little to the conversation during dinner, preferring to listen instead. But although she
remained alert to every nuance, every inflection of
Sam's contributions, she found nothing that
would prove concretely that he was playing the
diplomatic game of saying what the listener wanted
to hear. Or using a lot of profound statements to
say absolutely nothing. To her surprise he had
given frank answers to every question, promisng
no easy solutions. Very often his opinions had
been diametrically opposed to her own, yet they
had still contained the solid ring of truth.

She was still puzzling over his motivation when
Mr. Apperly rose to speak. After listening to his
loud, aimless speech for several minutes, Angie
fought against a face-contorting yawn, then caught
her breath in shock when she felt a large hand come
to rest on her left thigh. She cut her eyes swiftly
toward Sam. He was staring at the speaker, his
face set in lines of intense concentration, his left
hand resting on the table. But his right hand was
very definitely on her thigh.

Looking nervously around the room, she cau-
tiously inched her hand toward the edge of the
table, then glanced at Sam just as he turned his
head toward her. Suddenly time stopped as she
was singed by the desire blazing in his eyes. He
held her gaze for long, electric moments while heat

radiated outward from his hand to spread irresistibly through her body. His fingers remained motionless, but even when he turned away to focus his gaze on the speaker once more, the warmth caressed, holding her still.

Occasionally, in the past, Angie had found herself faced with a similar situation—a sly hand on her knee, a carefully planned grazing of her breast with a seemingly careless hand—and always before she had considered the surreptitious advances crude. But there was nothing crude about the look in Sam's eyes or the myriad emotions that were coursing through her body. It was a symphony of the most incredibly erotic sensations she had ever experienced.

The hand remained immobile as though he were unaware of the chaotic feelings that shook her. It simply lay there, exciting her imagination, stimulating needs a bolder caress would have squelched. a weighty languor suffused her body, her eyelids drooping slightly to give her a sleepy, sensual look, and her breasts trembled slightly with each indrawn breath.

The hectic throbbing of her pulse became concentrated in the erogenous parts of her body. Her breasts—so far from the tantalizing hand—and her loins—so excruciatingly near—pulsated in unison with her heated blood. And gradually the warm, still hand became a delicious torment. Every thought, every nerve became unswervingly fixed on it, willing it to move, to slide beneath the silken barrier to discover the fire he had built.

At the exact moment she felt she could no longer remain quiet, that she would scream in frustration if he didn't expand the caress, his fingers began to move slowly up her thigh. She caught her breath as her flesh began to sing wildly in anticipation, then, incredibly, the room was filled with applause. She looked around with glazed eyes, thinking for one crazy moment everyone was cheering the fact that his fingers had finally moved, only to find the speech was over and the spell broken.

Raising his hands to join in the tribute to Mr. Apperly's unheard speech, Sam glanced at her from the corners of brown eyes sparkling with desire and she swallowed nervously before adding her hesitant applause to the rest.

The first awards passed by in a haze of confusion, but gradually her senses returned and she was caught between anger at his having evoked private emotions in an extremely public place, and amusement at the thought of the respected, conservative senator acting with such audacity.

She watched silently as the remainder of the awards were presented, calmly waiting for the ceremony to end to blast him for his temerity. And although she fully expected to be caught in conversation for hours afterward, he deftly sidestepped any prolonged discussion and they were soon sitting in his car driving out of the parking lot.

"Now," she said firmly, shifting in her seat to face him. "Do you want to explain yourself, Senator?" Catching his guileless look, she added, "Don't pretend you don't know what I mean. What made you think I wanted a hundred people to watch me breathing heavy?"

"Were you breathing heavy, Angel?"

His voice was soft and sensual and she had to tighten her muscles to prevent a shiver from racing down her spine. "That's not the point," she hedged. "That was a dumb stunt."

Glancing at her, his lips twisted in the crooked smile that was becoming so familiar—and much too enjoyable to watch. "I'm sorry," he said, sounding not in the least bit sorry. "Charles is a good friend, but he could put a rabid dog to sleep. So"— he looked at her and shrugged, his face serious, his lip twitching in amusement—"when my mind started to wander, my hand just followed it."

"Your—" she sputtered incredulously, then burst out laughing. "You're terrible."

Pulling into a small, well-lit parking lot, he switched off the engine, then leaned his forearm on the steering wheel as he turned to look at her. "This is the first time I've seen you laugh—really laugh," he said, staring at her smiling face. "Before it was always a kind of reluctant chuckle. This is the first time you've relaxed your guard enough to be completely natural with me."

She opened her mouth to deny his statement, but found herself suddenly trapped in the warmth of his eyes. Shifting her gaze uncomfortably, she said, "Where are we? Why did you stop here?"

"Did you really think I would waste my whole evening with you on that public feeding? Especially since I have this overpowering feeling that it may be my only chance to captivate you with my charm." He smiled down at her, his eyes gentle, as though he had read her thoughts and understood her determination to keep him at arm's length. "Now we're going to get to know one another." He indicated the small building beside the parking lot and before she could voice a protest or form a question, he was out of the car and walking around it to open her door.

Relax and enjoy. It's only for tonight, she reminded herself as they walked into the small, dark club.

When they were seated at a lantern-lit table with drinks in hand, she stared at him curiously in the flickering shadows. "So tell me all about Senator Sam Clements. Did you want to conquer the world from the cradle or was it something you acquired along the way? And what exactly was the attraction? Power? Big bucks?"

He lifted her hand from the table, turning it to cradle it snugly in his palm, and stared down at her long fingers, then raised his eyes slowly as though fascinated by their joined hands. "What do you think?" he said quietly.

"Oh, no. This is supposed to be get-to-know-each-other time. You tell me," she admonished. "You know from my rambling in the cave that I think in open loops—come to think of it, my life is pretty much an open loop. Now it's your turn."

As he released her hand to pick up his drink, she felt suddenly cold and bit her lip in anger at her traitorous senses, waiting silently for him to taste his bourbon before he answered.

"When I was a boy, I did all the boy things and dreamed all the boy dreams. I wanted to be a fireman and a veterinarian and even a cowboy, but nothing as dull as a senator." He smiled across at her. "But boys grow up and turn into men."

"Do you mean that when puberty set in you knew automatically that you wanted to run the country?"

"Not exactly," he chuckled. "I began to study

law reluctantly. I knew it wasn't exactly what I wanted, but on the other hand, I didn't know exactly what it was that I *did* want. I slid into politics almost by mistake and when I did, I knew. It's as simple as that. But it wasn't power or money that hooked me. It was the excitement, the feeling of being in on history as it's being made." Grimacing, he added, "Maybe that's a form of power, but not in the way you mean. Most people have a very dim view of what actually goes on in our government. The average person feels frustrated because he or she can see what's wrong with the country, but is helpless to do anything about it. If you'll multiply that feeling a thousand times you might approach the frustration we in government feel. We're in decision-making positions, but can still do nothing concrete. We trudge along an inch at a time, hoping the decisions we make today will make some small difference in the future."

Oh Senator, she thought cynically, you've got the dedicated look down to a tee. The fervent light of truth is almost blinding. Where was the chink in his armor? He was too good to be true. In this day and age, no politician was that real. Avoiding his eyes she reached into her purse for a cigarette, but found her hand caught.

"You're hiding again," he said softly. "Whenever I say or do something that touches the real you, you bring out the hard shell, the skepticism." He looked at her thoughtfully. "I wonder what I said that got too close to the softness in you." He stood, pulling her to her feet. "Come and dance with me, Angel. Put away the shell."

"You don't think I have a right to be skeptical?"

she asked. As they reached the small wooden dance floor, she tried desperately to avoid thinking of the way his hands on her hips were sending signals she wasn't ready to receive.

"About politics in general, sure. About me in particular, why should you? Have you ever caught me with my hand in the cookie jar?"

It was a valid question, but if she answered it honestly, she would have to admit her doubt was the only weapon she had against his magnetism. She refused to speculate on why it was so important that she fight him. And so she ignored his question, concentrating on the music instead until an overenthusiastic couple bumped into her, causing her to step squarely on Sam's polished leather shoes.

"Sorry," she chuckled, watching over his shoulder as the pair swooped by to collide sharply with the unsuspecting dancers behind them.

Angie glanced up to share her amusement with Sam, then as she was held by the flame burning bright and steady in his eyes, her knees went weak from the force of his all-too-obvious desire and once again she trod heavily on his foot.

Pulling away from him in exasperation, she stopped dancing. "Lord, Sam. I'm sorry. I should have warned you to take out accident insurance before you dance with me."

He pulled her back against his chest and murmured in her ear, "Don't worry about it." He paused and his voice changed curiously. "Anyway, I think I'm beginning to like it."

The wry, puzzled note in his voice was so unexpected that she threw back her head and laughed without inhibition, placing her hands casually on his shoulders as she relaxed her guard completely.

He watched her face for a moment, a bemused expression passing across his features as he examined her smile, the twinkle in her gray eyes, then, slowly, he began to move her body in time to the soft love song.

Angie had no awareness of the time passing as she leaned against him comfortably. Their bodies seemed to have melded spiritually as well as physically and it felt as though they had always danced, had always been in perfect rhythm.

Suddenly she realized they were no longer moving, but standing in a dark corner behind a row of plants, hidden from the rest of the room. She raised her head as Sam's hands began sliding over her back and buttocks in spine-tingling, seductively elusive caresses. "Sam," she murmured huskily, unconscious of the way her body was arching into his. "I think your mind is wandering again."

"What mind?" he whispered hoarsely against her neck. "My mind has gone on vacation. I can't think of anything except the way you looked last night."

She sucked in her breath sharply, the desire in his deep voice and mobile hands sending a languorous warmth on an erotic trip through her body. It sapped her strength, disarming sensible thought.

Leaning against the wall in their dark corner, he pulled her to him tightly, trapping her hands against his chest, then raised his head to tease her ear with gentle nips and flicks of his tongue. "The picture of my hands on your body is driving me crazy," he groaned. "Your breasts, so round and full . . . I could feel them swelling under my hands, the nipples pushing tight and hard against my palms. . . . And for me, Angel—all for me."

His large hands cupped her buttocks, urging her closer to the proof of his desire. Her eyelids drifted shut, refusing to listen to the remnants of sanity that fought against the seduction of his touch, as did the slim hand that slipped beneath his jacket to steal the warmth from his body.

"It was the most incredible thing I've ever felt," he whispered roughly. His mouth descended to the taut tendons in her neck and she felt the tickling of his firm lips, the heat of his breath as he spoke. Her body ached with awareness. "I want to feel your nipples grow taut under my tongue, Angel, to suck them deep in my mouth. I want to taste and touch all of you. Last night only gave me a damnably tormenting hint of what it could be like."

A long, low sigh passed her lips as he pressed her ever closer. Drugged by his deep voice and the exquisite pictures he painted, she gave in to the sensations that vibrated through her, shivering uncontrollably in anticipation.

"There was a fine line of golden hair on your stomach that begged me to follow it to the sweetness," he whispered, pulling her further into his erotic dream. "I want that sweetness, Angel. I want to taste it, to touch your moist warmth. I want to fill up your softness with my strength, to feel it surrounding me until I'm lost in the pleasure of you."

His hands curved up and around her shoulders, probing the delicate collarbone, his touch growing frenzied in stunning coordination with her thoughts.

For a vision was growing behind her closed eyelids. She saw the two of them as they had stood the night before in her living room. But now instead of breaking apart, Sam dropped to his knees before her, burying his face in her smooth, rounded stomach. She could see herself sliding her fingers through his curly hair to grasp his head and pull him closer. She could feel herself arching into him. She could feel him touching her, loving her . . .

"What is it, Angel?" he whispered hoarsely. "What do you see?"

Lifting her eyelids to reveal drugged, bedazzled eyes, she stared at him for long moments, then shook her head to clear away the saturating fog of desire. She tried to move away, but his hands on her hips held fast. Meeting his eyes, she gave a husky, breathless laugh. "You're a dangerous man, Sam," she murmured. "I'm drunk. Give me no tongue twisters to repeat. No white lines to walk or balloons to blow up because I'd fail miserably. Completely, totally spiflicated am I." She leaned her head weakly on his chest. "Lord! That's the first time I've received an obscene phone call without a telephone."

He laughed softly against the top of her head, ruffling her fine hair as he rubbed his face across it in a rough caress. He hugged her tightly as though a secret joy were spilling over.

"Sam," she whispered. "I'm not equipped for this kind of thing. I don't know how to play sophisticated games."

She felt him stiffen suddenly, then his hands

framed her face and he pulled her head up, pinning her with the intensity of his gaze. "It's not a game, Angel. I've never been more serious in my life."

He released her to run one hand quickly through his hair, drawing in a slow, painful breath. "Come on, let's go," he muttered and turned to walk to their table for her purse, pulling her along as he then headed for the exit.

In the car Angie held her silence, desperately fighting to pull her battle-torn emotions together. It was quite a while before she felt composed enough to glance through the darkness in his direction.

He held his body stiff and the hands that gripped the steering wheel were white-knuckled. She stared at his rigid face as the passing streetlights highlighted the high brow with its errant lock of curly hair, the strong nose with nostrils compressed as if in pain, and she wondered incredulously if he were angry or could possibly have been affected as deeply as she.

Suddenly he gave a deep, shuddering sigh and she could feel his tension melting away. He glanced across at her and this time the crooked smile held a hint of self-mockery.

"Sam," she asked hesitantly. "Where are we going?"

He glanced around, seeming to come suddenly to the realization that they were on the interstate headed west. Laughing wryly, he said, "I don't have the foggiest notion." He cut his gaze sideways and suddenly misty gray eyes melted into warm brown ones as his voice softened perceptibly. "I just didn't want to take you home."

"Oh," she said softly, her mouth retaining the surprised shape of the word for seconds longer than necessary. She cleared her throat reflexively. "It's not that I would mind a trip to California, Sam, but unfortunately I have to work tomorrow."

He chuckled softly and eased the steering wheel to exit the highway. "That's too bad," he said regretfully. "I'd like to show you San Francisco." He paused, then added quietly, "Maybe next time."

Maybe next time. The words lingered in her mind on the drive to her apartment. There wasn't supposed to be a next time. She had definitely made up her mind about that, but somehow the thought brought no pleasure, no satisfaction.

Logically she knew that allowing the relationship to continue and grow was wrong. Even if she had not been singed by the enormous ego of a minor politician, she had seen enough of them in her line of work to know that her career, her lifetime goals would suffer in the long run. So maybe she hadn't found the falseness in his character tonight. It was there. It had to be. And even if it weren't, a sincere politician was still a politician. She had worked too hard to let her plans slide away from her now. Sam could sway her emotions without even trying hard. The burning flame of ambition was all too easily extinguished by the sensations that flooded her body when she was in his arms.

All these things she knew without a doubt. So why did the thought of not seeing him again cause a sudden constriction in her chest? Why did it bring an emptiness that was almost painful?

Glancing up, Angie found they had pulled into the parking space beside her Chevrolet and she hurried out of the car, but on the path to her door his hand suddenly descended on her neck, slowing her steps as though he were still trying to prolong the evening.

While she drew out her key, he leaned against the wall, capturing her hand as soon as she had unlocked the door. With his other hand he cupped her gently sloping jaw, running his thumb hypnotically across her cheekbone. "You still don't trust me, do you, Angel?" His large thumb moved to the corner of her mouth, parting her lips with a subtle pressure. "I want you," he said softly, then his voice grew strangely wistful as he added, "I'll have you, too. Never doubt that. It may take a while, but you'll come to me willingly—with no reservations."

Bowing his head, he brushed his lips back and forth across hers in a disquietingly tantalizing caress, then slid his hand to her neck and held her lips firmly against his as though trying to fuse her flesh with his. He withdrew slowly, reluctantly, and rested his forehead against hers with a softly whispered, "Goodnight, Angel." Then he turned and walked away, his hands shoved deep in the pockets of his slacks.

Five

Angie slammed the heavy volume shut and stood in exasperation. The pile of research books that lay before her on the coffee table needed attention. The more she learned about her subject, the more her excitement over the project grew. Pat was right. This book would cause a stir. And the authors would become overnight celebrities. So why in hell couldn't she keep her mind on the subject? Why did that blasted crooked smile keep drifting into her head?

She began to pace up and down, running her fingers irritably through her fine, silver hair.

Every thought, every doubt she had had about Sam was being proven true. He was disrupting her life—and she hadn't seen him in over two weeks, damn his eyes! From a televised news conference she had learned of his return to Washington, but the distance between them didn't seem to make any difference. It was positively spooky the way he crept into her head, constantly pulling her thoughts away from her work.

At times she told herself that he had forgotten her, given up his pursuit as not worth the effort. Then she would remember the determined gleam in his eyes, the soft stroke of steel in his voice when she had last seen him. No, he hadn't given up. He would be back. It was only a matter of time.

Angie very much resented the fact that he had chosen to enter her life at a time when she needed all her concentration, all her strength to carry her through the crisis in her career. The next few months would be a turning point for her and she would need all her wits to simply get through them, much less come out on top.

"And when I do choose to have an affair," she muttered testily, "it won't be with some honey-tongued politician."

She was well on her way to working herself into a full-fledged fury when the doorbell rang, cutting sharply into her ricocheting thoughts. Tightening the belt of her dusty rose wraparound robe, she walked to the door and threw it open, taking out part of her frustration on the innocent wood.

"Pat!" she cried, relief at the diversion overriding her surprise. "What are you doing here? I thought you were interviewing Faraday tonight."

"Don't mention that louse to me," he growled, pushing her aside to walk into the living room and flop heavily onto the couch. "He's clammed up on me again. Every time we reach a vital point in his recollections, the man sinks into a deep, dark, *silent* hole. It's the most maddening—" He clenched his teeth in fury, punched a throw pillow, then turned to look at Angie standing in front of him. "I don't want to talk about it. Tonight I want to forget Michael Faraday even exists."

"But if he refuses to talk—"

"I don't want to talk about it," he repeated. He removed his shoes, pushed her books aside, and propped his feet comfortably on the low wicker coffee table. "Besides that's what you're for. To get all the stuff out of him that won't come out for me. And don't forget the meeting tomorrow night. It'll be relatively boring, but since he'll be speaking, you should get some insights into his character."

"Will I be able to talk with him afterward?" Callously she shoved his large feet off the table and sat beside him.

"I doubt it." Leaning his head back with a sigh, he opened one eye to look at her. "Now can we drop it? Entertain me. Take my mind off that melancholy dinosaur."

"What do you suggest?" she asked drily. "I gave up the belly-dancing lessons when I threw my hip out of joint."

He rolled his head sideways and smiled sweetly. "Sex is the only thing that consistently takes my mind off my problems."

"How about a game of checkers?"

"Sex," he insisted, raising his large frame to lean forward.

She jumped off the couch, chuckling at the evil leer on his face. "Behave yourself. Have you had dinner?"

"Sex," he repeated, his voice taking on the monotone of one of the living dead, and stood to walk toward her, his arms extended limply.

"Pat!" she laughed, dodging as he lunged drunkenly. She squealed in surprise as he caught her off guard and threw her back onto the couch, falling heavily on top of her.

"Patrick Denby, get off," she gasped, laughing uncontrollably as he nuzzled her neck with loud snorting kisses. "You weigh a ton."

Grabbing his bushy hair with one hand, she held his head away from her neck, breaking into fresh laughter when he grinned idiotically, unconcerned that his head hung there in mid-air. She gave his head a shake, then threw him a startled look when the sound of the doorbell once again filled the living room.

She rolled sideways as Patrick eased away from her and straightened her robe before walking to the door. Smoothing her hair with one hand, she opened the door with the other, then stood paralyzed, her eyes widening in surprise when she saw who was standing there.

"Sam!" she gasped, looking nervously over her shoulder at Patrick. She could tell by his raised brows that his reporter's brain was already clicking away furiously. Turning back to Sam, she said hesitantly, "I—I didn't know you were back."

"May I come in?" He spoke softly, his eyes drifting over her disheveled figure, then moving on to take in Pat whose shirt had come unbuttoned in their struggles.

"Of course. Do you know Patrick Denby?" She glanced at Pat, imploring him silently to refrain from commenting on Sam's presence.

"We've met," Sam murmured, extending his hand. "Good to see you again, Denby."

"Same here, Senator." Pat shook the proffered hand, then sat casually on the arm of the couch, staring up at Sam. "I see I should have questioned Ange more carefully after you were trapped in the cave. Very often people—people who get to know one another in a stressful situation—feel a bond that draws them to each other." He eyed them casually. "Of course, sometimes it works in reverse and they avoid seeing people they've met under those circumstances because it tends to remind them of a bad time in their lives. Obviously Ange here doesn't remind you of almost being blown to bits."

"Thank you, Professor Denby," Angie said sarcastically, breaking into the tension growing between the two men. "Now that we've thoroughly explored the emotions of people in a stressful situation, perhaps we can move on to something more pleasant—like your departure."

"But Angela," Patrick said mournfully. "You were going to entertain me."

"That was before we found we couldn't agree on the form of entertainment," she said between clenched teeth.

Looking up at her with his sad, bloodhound eyes, he said, "You offered to feed me. I haven't had my dinner."

"*Pat*," she said in a low, threatening voice, conscious of Sam's watchful eyes.

"Look, love, you won't have to do a thing," Pat coaxed. "The senator and I will go out for pizza and beer."

"No!" Angie bit her lip as the vehemence of her

objection caused Sam to look at her with raised brows. "I mean, the senator may have other plans."

Sam said nothing for a moment, holding her eyes until she shifted uncomfortably, then said quietly, "Why don't you ask *the senator*?"

"Sure," Pat said enthusiastically. "You leave all the details to us. Why don't you go and throw a salad together and we'll be back in a flash with the trash." He stepped into his shoes and looked over his shoulder at Angie, his expression hidden from Sam. "I'm sure we'll find *heaps* of things to talk about."

I'll just bet you will, you fink, she thought, her eyes narrowing at the gleeful look on his face, but before she could corner him the two men were walking out the door.

In the kitchen she tore viciously at a head of lettuce, pretending it was Patrick's precious beard. She didn't want Pat to question Sam—about their relationship or anything else. Pat had too much integrity to sell to the gossip papers, but she wouldn't put it past him to do a story on Sam just for the fun of it. Everyone in the country was in love with Sam Clements and the more sensationalist weeklies would have dearly loved to get their hot little hands on inside information concerning his personal life.

She paused in her fuming to change into jeans and sweat shirt, then returned to her assault on the vegetables. The tomato she held in her hand was saved from becoming tomato puree only by the sound of the front door opening. Glancing at the clock, she realized she had been standing there lecturing the salad for over thirty minutes.

"Time sure flies when you're contemplating murder," she muttered, then as she heard a burst of raucous laughter, she stuck her head around the door to peer warily into the living room, checking Sam's expression quickly for any signs of anger. She breathed a silent sigh of relief when she saw Patrick slap Sam good-naturedly on the back.

"By God, Ange," Pat chuckled, glancing toward the kitchen. "Why didn't you tell me Sam was such a prince of a fellow?"

"Didn't I mention that?" she asked, meeting Sam's laughter-filled eyes. "I was sure I had." Crossing the room, she linked her arms with theirs. "Come on, Prince—and you too, Pauper. The salad has had a tough night. I think it's time to put it out of its misery."

"Hey, Ange," Pat said as they walked into the kitchen. "Are you putting on the dog?"

She lifted an inquiring brow when he indicated her second-best plastic dinnerware on the table.

"All your plates match," he said in surprise. "You should feel honored, Sam. She makes me eat off paper towels."

"We must pay homage to the office if not the man," she replied primly, then turned away and fanned her face furiously when she felt Sam's hand slip down below her waist to curve around her jean-clad buttocks.

"Indeed, indeed," Sam agreed, grinning at her impudently as he flipped open the pizza box and grabbed a large slice. He turned his chair around to straddle it, propping his forearms on the back as he ate.

Angie sat down and eyed the two men as they

swallowed beer and pizza without pause. "You're pigs," she said slowly.

"True," Pat mumbled through a mouthful of salad. "Isn't it lucky we're sexy enough to make up for it?"

She started to ignore his outrageous comment, but when Sam gave Pat a startled look and choked on his beer, a chuckle escaped her, growing into unrestrained laughter when Pat sent her an offended look.

From that moment on the evening became an uproarious free-for-all, the beer and laughter flowing with equal freedom. It no longer seemed strange to see the world-famous senator trading tall stories with her unkempt, unrecognized friend.

At ten o'clock, as Sam finished the hilarious saga of a frog he'd owned at age ten, Partrick rose to leave. "You may be a lady of leisure now," he said as Angie walked him to the door, "but I'm still making payments to two ex-wives." He glanced at Sam who had followed them into the living room. "Expensive things, wives."

"So I've heard," Sam chuckled.

At the door Pat enveloped Angie in a crushing bear hug, kissing her noisily before turning to Sam. "I'm glad you dropped by, Sam. It's taught me something—some politicians really do resemble human beings after all." With that he walked out the door, leaving Angie to face the uncomfortable silence that had been growing since Pat announced he was leaving.

"Lady of leisure?" he asked as she stood by the door playing with the bottom of her sweatshirt.

"As of yesterday," she said quietly, nodding her head. "I'm starting a project that will take

77

up most of my time, so we thought it would be best."

His eyes narrowed at the word "we," but he didn't question its use. He merely sat down and asked quietly, "I hope I didn't interrupt anything in coming here tonight?"

Angie's gaze sharpened at his strange tone. He was smiling, but something was wrong. His jacket and tie had been long ago discarded and his shirt was open at the neck, the familiar lock of hair was resting once again on his forehead. But he looked tired, and his skin seemed a little gray under his healthy tan. Yet it wasn't his weariness that made her catch her breath. Beneath his smiling, casual expression she saw hurt.

Damn him! she thought angrily, as she found herself more affected than was comfortable. What right does he have to be hurt? Why should he come in here looking like I've wounded him—like I've treated him badly? His pain made her feel guilty, which in turn made her more furious.

"Did you miss me?"

His quiet voice broke into her mute tirade, bringing her head up sharply. She wiped her palms on her jeans, walking closer as she murmured a distracted, "What?"

"I asked if you missed me," he repeated patiently. "I didn't get in touch with you on purpose, thinking you would miss me so badly you would throw yourself into my arms when I returned." He sighed with exaggerated regret. "I guess if you want something done right"—reaching out, he grasped her by the waist, pulling her across the arm of the couch into his lap—"you simply have to do it yourself," he finished with gentle determination against the side of her neck.

"Sam," she said, pushing against his massive chest. "Sam! This is ridiculous. You don't have to prove anything. I'll freely admit that I missed you. Now let me go."

"Yes," he said, laughing shortly as he increased the pressure on her waist. "I saw how much you missed me. You missed me so much, you took up with a grizzly bear while I was gone." He ran his hands up her body to grip her shoulders, and lowered her to the couch. "You don't need him, Angel. You don't even want him. I'll show you what you want."

"You hard-headed jackass," she hissed, arching her body to try and shove him off. "If you'll listen to me . . ."

But he moved into her just as she arched her body, covering her mouth fiercely with his own, and Fourth of July fireworks began exploding in her head, rocketing wildly through her veins.

He was right. This was what she wanted, what she had dreamed of, fought against for two weeks. Parting her lips with a sigh, she slid her arms around his waist and gave herself up to the exquisite sensation.

Somehow when he was close to her like this, with his hard, strong body pressing into hers, she couldn't quite remember why she was fighting him. What could possibly be more important than the consuming need he brought with his touch? The beauty of the feelings racing through her body, the rightness, the warmth, overwhelmed her.

He grasped a handful of hair at the back of her

head to hold her close, plunging his tongue deep into the moist sweetness of her mouth, greedily taking what she wanted so desperately to give.

Drawing back a fraction of an inch, he whispered against her lips, his breath a hot caress on the sensitive flesh. "You see how it is? Tell me you feel this with anyone else."

He extended his tongue, leisurely outlining her lips, tormenting her, frustrating her urgent need to feel his firm mouth on hers. When he heard the moan begin deep in her throat, he closed the gap, the fierceness of the brief kiss bringing a welcome pain.

"Tell me." He groaned.

"No one." She gasped, her body arching convulsively beneath him. "It's never been . . . I've never wanted . . ."

She couldn't continue. Her mind wouldn't stay on the subject long enough to form the words. Her thoughts kept wandering to the hard body beneath his clothing.

When his hands descended to capture her aching breasts, she almost screamed with an agonizing mixture of relief and pleasure, moving her body frenetically into the pressure of his massaging fingers. She slid her hands to his taut buttocks, pressing her fingers into the hard flesh, showing him the urgency of her desire.

It was only when he slowly withdrew his lips that Angie became aware of the ringing. Looking up at him with sensually drugged eyes, she tried to take in what the ringing meant. She knew it should have some meaning, but the only thing that made sense was the aching want, the throbbing desire he had built in her groin.

From a great distance she watched as he picked up the telephone and murmured a gruff "Hello." Then his eyes began to change, the fire dying slowly as he handed her the receiver.

"It's Denby," he said and stiffly raised himself to stand beside the couch with his back to her.

She raised the receiver to her ear reluctantly. She could hear Patrick speaking, but couldn't seem to take in his words as she watched Sam run fingers that trembled through his curly hair, then move to pick up his discarded jacket.

"I'll call you tomorrow," she murmured huskily, replacing the phone quickly as Sam began to walk toward the door.

"Sam?"

He turned back and stared at her inquiringly, weariness adding deep lines to his strong face.

Moving over to the window, she gazed out into the dark night with concentrated intensity as though it were necessary to memorize everything she saw there.

"Pat and I are just friends," she began reluctantly. She couldn't understand why she was explaining the situation to Sam. She only knew that she had to. And the fact that it was so important made her uncomfortable, causing her voice to become stiff and stilted as she continued. "We're working on a project together, the one I told you about. I mean"—she laughed shortly, glancing at him over her shoulder—"if I offered myself to him, he would make love to me. But only because I was there—he can't resist peanuts on a bar either."

Angie watched in fascination as his eyes began to change once again. A spark of something indefinable flicked to life, growing steadily until it became a blazing sable fire and—as though he had swallowed a magic elixir—the weary lines disappeared.

He moved toward her, speaking in a soft, lazy voice. "Well I'd say that clears up how Denby feels. What about you?"

"Me?" she asked in surprise. "He's a friend. I like him. Period. I've never felt any overwhelming urges when I'm with him. Not like—" She broke off, biting her lip as she returned her gaze to the dark night.

She heard him move to stand behind her, then felt his hand on her shoulder as he turned her around, linking his hands behind her neck.

"Not like what, Angel?" He rested his forehead against hers, forcing her to meet his eyes. "Not like when you're with me. Isn't that what you were going to say?"

"No," she said, offering the blatant lie belligerently.

"Why did you feel it necessary to explain?" he asked, his soft words holding a hint of smugness. "Why did you want me to know the truth?"

"You son of a . . ."

Before she could finish the curse, his lips stopped her with a brief, hard kiss. "I thought I told you not to swear," he murmured.

He was so close, the touch of his breath on her face caused her lips to twitch traitorously. Then her eyes darkened to steel as she took in the soft command, her face frozen in stiff, stubborn lines.

"Damn," she said deliberately.

This time his mouth stayed longer, punishing her hard-headedness with the subtly seductive movement of his lips against hers. Her eyelids drifted down, a reluctant sigh of pleasure escaping her parted lips as he pulled back slowly.

She lifted her weighted eyelids and stared at him with misty, bewitched eyes. "Hell," she whispered, her voice husky with desire.

Chuckling softly, he covered her lips again in triumph, then pulled her close to hug her enthusiastically. He moved his lips across her cheekbone and nipped gently at her ear. "It surprises you as much as it does me, doesn't it. This feeling that blossoms every time we touch. It's the damndest thing," he whispered huskily against her neck. "When I'm away from you, there's always something nagging at me. I know that I need to be with you." He laughed shakily. "But then when I hold you, the explosion—the breath-stealing burst of feeling—it floors me all over again." His voice held amazement and awe as he added, "I honestly didn't know a thing like this was possible."

He closed his eyes tightly for a moment as though trying to contain some fierce emotion, then opened them to look down at her. "I know you feel the same thing, Angel. But I also know it doesn't please you the way it does me." When she started to speak, he stopped her with a finger on her lips. "It's all right. I understand. The whole thing's a little confusing for me, too. It's hard to trust something that hits you so suddenly and with such intensity. And I know you feel it would disrupt your life if you gave in to it."

His voice was soft and caring and compassionate. And if he had asked her to go to the moon with him at that moment, she would have started looking for lead-weighted boots. But he didn't. He rubbed his rough cheek against hers and said,

"We've got plenty of time. As long as I know you'll give it a fair chance to work, I can wait."

His hand tightened on her shoulders as though the words were difficult to say and regretted immediately, then he sucked in his breath and said, "Can I see you tomorrow night?"

Her nod of affirmation was halted almost before it began. "I can't," she said, her voice sounding thin and much too regretful. "I have to go to a meeting with Pat. It's research for the thing we're doing together."

"No problem," he said in unconcern. "I'll come too."

"But you can't," she protested. "It's a meeting of radicals . . . protesters . . . dissidents. Not exactly the kind of thing a politician should be seen attending."

"I go where I want and do what I want, Angel," he explained patiently. "I didn't change my values to fit the government; I'm trying to change the government to fit my values. But if you're really worried about my image, I'll simply let my people know what I'm doing. If it's all out in the open, there won't be any repercussions."

"Are you sure?" she asked doubtfully, trying to picture Sam mingling with the unconventional characters who would be attending the meeting tomorrow. "This won't be a group of citizens banding together to try and solve our country's problems. These people are actively fighting the government, in any way they can."

"I'm positive. Now is it a date?"

She shrugged helplessly. "Sure. Why not? My favorite fantasy is having a date with two men at the same time." She paused, thoughtfully tugging at her ear. "Of course, I never imagined the two men would be Gene Autrey and Gabby Hayes, but I'm adaptable."

His laughter lingered long after he was gone, warming her against her will well into the night.

Angie glanced back as Sam ushered her into the small, badly lit meeting hall. She still couldn't take in the change in his appearance. Drawing in a secret breath of pleasure, she let her eyes roam over the tight, well-worn jeans that hugged his muscular thighs, then moved her gaze up to the navy blue shirt, open deep at the throat, exposing the mat of curling hair on his broad chest, the sleeves rolled up to show strong, tanned forearms.

God, he's gorgeous, she thought as she reluctantly pulled her gaze away to search for Pat. After spotting him at the front of the hall, she and Sam found seats nearer the exit and sat down to wait for Michael Faraday to appear.

On the drive from her apartment she had filled Sam in on the purpose of the research she was doing with Pat. Sam had, of course, recalled Michael Faraday and had been able to give her some astonishingly perceptive insights into the events of an era that she only vaguely remembered.

Gradually the murmur of voices in the hall dwindled until there was total silence. Pulling her miniscule tape recorder from her purse, she craned her neck to see the man seated on a small platform at the front of the room.

His appearance had changed drastically from the last time she had seen him. The headband and rumpled clothing had been discarded, leaving a thin, distinguished older man. Although he still didn't have the corporate look, his hair was neatly trimmed, his lean, craggy face clean shaven.

"In the beginning there was the rock."

He began to speak quietly, with no preface, and to her surprise his voice was soft and compelling, his words showing an educated background. As he spoke of the history of United States involvement in foreign affairs, she found he was not only intelligent, but possessed a sharp, logical mind. The logic, however, seemed to her to be rather simplistic, not allowing for human variances, and his solutions too general to be of any real use.

Whispers from the seats directly in front of her caused Angie to lean forward to try and catch the softly spoken words. It was at this point in his talk that something seemed to slip in Faraday's mind. His words became slurred and urgent. He seemed to be proposing a garbled version of the end justifying the means or the sacrifice of a few for the good of the many.

It didn't make sense and Angie looked at Sam in confusion. He was staring at Faraday, his eyes filled with pity, then his gazed narrowed and grew sharp and she turned back to find the cause.

It didn't take her long to pinpoint the trouble. In the back of her mind she had recognized earlier the tension growing in the two rows of seats just below them. Now the tension had built to a low rumble of discontent.

She felt Sam shift in his seat and grab her arm, but it was too late. Before they could stand the first insult was hurled, touching a match to visibly heightened emotions. She never knew when the first punch was thrown or by whom, but suddenly Pat appeared and shoved his camera into her hands as the scuffle grew swiftly into a full-fledged brawl.

"Get pictures!" Pat shouted, grinning as he turned back to the fight.

Angie shook off Sam's hand and moved quickly out to the aisle for a better view. Photography was not her area of expertise, so she began swinging the camera around, snapping indiscriminately. She figured if she took enough pictures, some of them had to turn out right.

Ignoring the men rolling in the aisle at her feet, she recorded the vigorous disagreement as best she could. Through the noise she heard Sam calling her name, and shouted, "Just one more shot," then continued snapping.

Her knees buckled unexpectedly as two men rolled into her from behind, shoving her into a girl with long blond hair who was casually leaning against one of the seats, apparently undisturbed by the furor around them. Then suddenly one of the men who had rolled into Angie rose and tried to jerk the camera from her. She held on with both hands, kicking him viciously in the shin when he refused to let go. She had just managed to wrestle it away when she felt herself being pushed from behind and turned to give a small, startled man a sharp jab in the ribs, smiling smugly when she heard his grunt of pain. The strange person who seemed bent on owning Pat's camera looked as though he were about to renew his attack when Angie felt herself being lifted by the elbows and turned toward the exit.

"It's time we were leaving, Angel," Sam said, his voice calm as he bent to speak in her ear, his large frame shielding her from the noisy debate behind them.

She grinned up at him as he moved her toward the exit, then winced when a man came flying backward into them. He looked up into Sam's face, smiled good-naturedly, then doubled up his fist and drew back to invite Sam to participate in the festivities.

Angie sucked in her breath sharply, waiting helplessly for the blow to land, but Sam—his movements almost lazy—turned, caught the man's arm with his left hand as his right connected solidly with the man's chin, then continued moving her toward the door.

Before they reached the exit Angie glanced back over her shoulder, just in time to see Patrick's head above the crowd. He bellowed a rebel yell and dove head first into the swarm of bodies, a look of pure joy shining on his bearded face.

Outside, her eyes met Sam's. The two of them broke into spontaneous laughter and with clasped hands ran across the parking lot to the car as the fight began to spill out the door.

In the car Angie leaned back against the leather seat, trying to catch her breath. "Sam my boy," she sighed, laughter bubbling over in her voice, "you have got one mean right hook. Did you see the look on that guy's face when you decked him? He looked so surprised!"

Pulling her across the seat, Sam put his arm around her, his soft laughter stirring her hair. "He doesn't know it, but I was doing him a favor. If I had let you get at him, he could have been crippled for life."

Raising her head, she looked up into his laughing face and something fluttered inside her, causing her to catch her breath. *Oh, Senator,* she thought wryly, *what am I going to do with you?* She had known from the beginning she was attracted to him. Slowly, grudgingly, she had come to respect and admire him. Now something much more dangerous was happening. She was beginning to like him.

Six

In the next few weeks Angie felt as though she were trying to sustain a relationship with a jack-in-the-box. She saw Sam when he was in town and fought against missing him when he wasn't.

The way he dropped in and out of her life was driving her certifiably bonkers. When she was with him she wanted to grab him and shout, "Be still! You're making me seasick." He seemed to stay just long enough to build her desire to a frenzied peak, then he would fly off again to the land of Oz, leaving her frustrated and confused.

"That's what I get for letting myself become involved with a damned—" Even as the word left her mouth, her lips began to tingle crazily and she groaned, picking up her pencil to try to return to her work.

The research was progressing steadily, which

was astonishing considering the way Sam was constantly in her thoughts. She had had two meetings with Michael Faraday, but each had been brief and frustratingly unproductive. There was something about him. Something she couldn't put her finger on. Most of the time he had a keen, beautifully lucid mind, then for no apparent reason he slipped into an almost incoherent melancholy.

Pushing her notebook and tape recorder aside she leaned forward, resting her head on the cool table. The headache that had been growing steadily all day was now pounding painfully against the inside of her skull and her throat actually itched.

It was that blasted virus that was going around. It had to be. Diane, her next-door neighbor, had had it last week and Patrick the week before. It stood to reason that she would come down with it, too. Diane had told her yesterday that a scratchy throat was the first symptom and since then had been hovering like a penitent Florence Nightingale.

"I don't want to be sick," Angie moaned weakly, then stood slowly and went to the medicine cabinet for some time-release cold capsules. She swallowed them quickly before reaching for the thermometer. If there were any justice in the world, her temperature would be at least 109. Anything less would be a mockery of her aching body.

Sticking the thermometer in her mouth, she wrapped her arms around herself as a chill shook her violently. The comfortably battered sweater she wore had once belonged to her brother and reached down to mid-thigh. Its woolen folds should have kept her warm since it wasn't a cool day, but she felt as though each muscle in her body were shivering separately.

Shuffling into the living room, she groaned when she heard the doorbell. Diane had already given her enough homemade soup to supply the Salvation Army and Angie was very much afraid she would be violently ill if she saw one more Tupperware bowl full of the yellow muck.

She pulled the door open, then closed her eyes weakly when she saw Sam standing there. Opening one eye she watched as he examined first her pale face, disheveled hair, and the thermometer protruding from her mouth, then her comfortable, but threadbare jeans and the bright red wool socks covering her feet.

"You're ill."

"Lord, you're bright," she muttered under her breath, removing the thermometer. "My nose weighs three and a half pounds, my tongue has put on its winter underwear, teeny-tiny people are playing shuffleboard in my stomach, and the highway department is dynamiting a tunnel through my brain." She paused as though considering it. "Yes, you're right. I'm ill."

His laughter rang out deep and rich as he pulled her into his arms, cradling her head against his shoulder. "Oh Angel, what would I do without you? Lord, I've missed you."

She snuggled into the warmth of his body, rubbing her feverish face against his throat. "I feel so bad, Sam," she whispered weakly.

"Of course you do," he soothed, moving her toward the couch. "But I'm here now and I'll take care of you."

She sank onto the couch and curved her body into his, pulling her legs up behind her, sighing in relief as she relaxed against him. She was almost purring as the brown velvet voice began weaving its spell, mesmerizing her with tales of the new bill he was sponsoring and the dull parties he had endured during their separation. She knew he was hypnotizing her into relaxing, but she gave into the peace willingly.

Soon the words became lost in her head and she stared up at him, studying his face. She raised her hand slowly to touch the curly brown hair, then traced the strong, masculine nose with her index finger.

As her liquid gray eyes met his, she whispered profoundly, "Hi." But somehow her tongue tripped against her teeth and the word sounded slurred and drunken.

"Angel," he said softly. "You haven't by any chance been nipping at the cooking sherry, have you?"

"Cold capsules," she said, as though he knew of her susceptibility to medication of any kind and would automatically understand. Her finger followed the deep grooves on either side of his mouth and she smiled in pleasure at the hard, male beauty she saw in his face. "You're so damn cute and—and adorable."

"Cute and adorable?" he murmured in disgust. "Add green to that and you have Kermit the frog." He sighed as he kissed the top of her head. "I don't want you to find me cute and adorable; I want you to find me irresistible."

"I swore," she said to herself, then looked up at him. "Didn't you hear me swear?"

He chuckled in delight as he kissed her briefly, then lifted her into his arms and stood up. "Come on, love. Let's get you to bed."

"You, too?" she murmured drowsily, wrapping her arms around his neck.

"*Now* she invites me into her bed," he muttered as he carried her into the bedroom. "You have a lousy sense of timing, Angel."

When he stood her beside the bed and began removing her clothes, it never occurred to her to protest. This was Honest Sam and he had promised to take care of her. She sat on the bed when she heard him rummaging through the drawers of her bureau. Her foggy brain tried to grasp the strong sense of well-being that was seeping through her pores, but it was impossible to analyze. She knew the feeling centered around Sam, and a touch of something—apprehension perhaps—reached her before she gave up thinking as a useless occupation.

After he had slipped a gown over her head, he pushed her gently down on the pillow, tucking the cover snuggly around her body. Then she felt his lips brush across her forehead and she let the warmth of his caring soothe her into sleep.

Her throat felt like it had been dusted with sand when she awoke in the night. She felt a bare warm body beside her in the bed and smiled sleepily as she tried to move out from under the arm encircling her waist.

"What is it?" he murmured, his voice husky with sleep. He tightened his hold on her body as she tried again to move.

"I'm thirsty," she said softly.

"I'll get it. You stay where you are."

He rolled sideways and left the bed, returning seconds later with a glass of water.

After she had greedily emptied the glass, she peered hazily through the darkness at him. "Sam," she mumbled. "Are you supposed to be in my bed?"

Lifting the cover, he crawled back in beside her and took her in his arms. "Now, whose bed should I be in, if not yours?"

It made sense. In her drowsy, unguarded state—with no fences built around her emotions—it made all the sense in the world. She curled up against him, resting her head on his broad chest, and went back to sleep, convinced that all was right with the world.

Angie awakened slowly, letting morning seep into her brain at its leisure. The aching muscles and throbbing head were gone. In fact she felt wonderfully, marvelously alive, as though being ill had taught her how miraculous being well was.

She stretched in contentment, then when her hand encountered warm flesh, she opened her eyes and turned on her side, smiling as she gazed at his sleeping face.

Sam, she thought warmly. He had taken care of her last night. He had shown up just when she needed him and had let her lean on his strength.

Her eyes left his face and wandered down his bare chest, lingering on the thick mat of curling hair. Her fingers itched to touch him, to discover the hard lines of his body, to mold the strong flesh with her fingers. Why had it taken her so long to realize that this man was meant to be in her bed?

She watched in fascination as his chest expanded with a deeply indrawn breath and she jerked her gaze back to his face to find his eyes trained on her face.

"How do you feel?"

The quiet words were stiff, his voice tight and tense. Angie shook her head helplessly on the pillow. "I feel dizzy," she whispered. "But not from the virus; that's gone."

His eyes closed briefly as he exhaled in a powerful gust, then he propped himself up on one elbow and stared down at her. His hand shook slightly as it touched her face, lingering a second before moving down to slide the cover to her waist.

"It's time, isn't it?" he murmured hoarsely. "It's been a long, tough winter, but spring has finally arrived." He gave a shaky laugh. "And we're going to have a May Day celebration that will knock your socks off, Angel."

He stared down at her, not touching her, but simply following the curves under the thin gown and lower where the blanket only suggested her slim form. She held her breath, fascinated by the intensity of his gaze and the desire she heard in his husky whisper.

"Last night was the most exquisite torture I've ever endured," he whispered urgently. "It was enough to turn my hair gray." His eyes returned to her swelling breasts. "Since the first time we kissed, not a day has gone by that I didn't dream of seeing you as you were last night with your soft, ivory skin gleaming under my hands, and so willing, without an ounce of hesitation. A dream come true—and I couldn't lay a finger on you. No man should have to endure such torture."

He extended his hand to push the tiny straps off her shoulders, his fingers trembling slightly as though it took all his strength to go slowly. His hand followed the strap down her arm, then slid back up to her shoulder, then down again, his fingers playing across her flesh as though he were fascinated by the feel of her. His fingers dipped down to the top of her gown, the tips slid beneath it fleetingly, then turned away to her throat. They trailed softly up to her chin and back to the delicate V at the base of her throat, then dipped lower, grazing the tops of her rounded breasts before slipping away again.

The delicious torment was driving her wild and when he pushed the silky gown lower, she arched into the hand before it could retreat again, moaning in relief as it closed around one aching breast.

"It's good, isn't it, sweet?" he whispered as his hand slid beneath her breast to cup it gently, the large, rough thumb teasing the rosy tip until it stood taut and hard.

A fire was growing inside her, fanned into life by his touch, fueled by the strength of his desire, until it threatened to rage out of control. The blood was singing through her veins, stopping to throb at each pulse point and secret place. It was the most astounding sensation. Nothing she had ever felt could begin to compare with it.

And suddenly she knew the why of her existence. It was as though she were compelled to join with this man, as though everything that went before had been leading up to this incredible culmination.

A tremor shook her as he ran his hands down her body to slide the blanket away. Her gown was bunched up around her thighs and his breath became labored as he stared at her long, slender legs and the rounded curves barely covered by the thin nylon. Bending over her he began to push the fabric up, removing the gown slowly, tormenting them both with the leisurely pace.

With languid strokes he learned the feel of her ribs and her gently rounded stomach, grazing with a tantalizing caress the golden triangle of curls that held the heart of her pulsating desire. She moaned her need as his hand slipped down to part her legs and stroke the soft inner flesh of her thighs.

Her breath was coming in short, urgent gasps as an unfamiliar feeling began to build within her heated body, nagging at her, holding her poised on the edge of an unknown, irresistibly beckoning world.

Suddenly he dipped his head to latch on to one pebble-hard nipple, sucking it deep into his mouth, and at the same moment his large hand clasped the hot, moist mound between her thighs, opening and closing rhythmically.

"Sam," she moaned hoarsely, arching into the manipulating fingers, desperate for more and still more of him. "Sam, please!" Her breath felt incredibly hot on her lips as she opened her drugged eyes to plead for what they each craved.

"Lord!" he groaned and his head came up to crush her lips.

She grasped his neck with unsteady fingers as his mouth slanted across hers, devouring the sensitive flesh with a desperate hunger. She pushed her fingers through the thick, curly hair, holding him to her greedily as she moved her breasts urgently against his rough chest.

His tongue dipped deep into her mouth as though he searched for secrets, but instead of assuaging the ravenous hunger, it only increased their appetite. When he clasped her buttocks to pull her closer to his hard, throbbing need, she slid her hands beneath his shorts, massaging the smooth, hard flesh with frantic fingers, pushing the brief barrier away from his overheated skin.

He pulled back to discard the last remaining obstacle and she stared in fascination at the hard, lean body before her, running rapacious eyes over his broad, hair-covered chest, down the flat stomach and lean hips, following the line of hair as it narrowed then spread to surround his aroused masculinity.

She jerked her head up as he made a strange animal sound deep in his throat, then gasped at the raging desire that contorted his face and opened her arms to guide him home.

Their cries of ecstasy merged as he entered the moist, warm haven and claimed it as his own with increasingly urgent strokes. The erotic love words he whispered feverishly against her neck, the feel of his hard body against hers, the heated shaft that reached deep to the heart of her desire caused her to cry out her pleasure, groan her need.

At her cries, he increased the pace, each deep thrust bringing her closer and closer to a place she had only dreamed of before. Until, suddenly, she felt the incredible tension growing to enormous proportions, then wave after rippling wave of rapture shook her body and she gasped his name, gripping his shoulders frantically as he joined her in the explosive denouement.

Angie lay there for endless moments, her perspiration-soaked body filled with a delicious lassitude, her mind drugged with pleasure, and listened as his rough breathing returned to normal. Lifting a weighted hand she brushed the curls from the forehead that rested on her breast.

Feeling the touch, he moved his head back to look up at her, his eyes filled with an astonishing combination of emotions—contentment, gratitude and a deep, loving warmth.

She swallowed the lump in her throat and ran her finger down the strong line of his nose, then said in a voice ragged with the remnants of passion, "You'll do anything for a vote, won't you?"

The unexpected comment caused his shoulders to shake with delighted laughter and he abruptly rolled over onto his back, pulling her with him. "Angel, my angel," he murmured, his voice filled with laughter and a strange childlike joy. "Thank you for taking me to heaven."

"Is that where we went?" she asked softly. "I guess that's why I saw the stars close up."

"That's right," he confirmed, chuckling, then sighed in contentment. "Oh, Angel. I must have done something very good in my life to deserve today." He reached up to touch her fine hair. "My silver-haired angel. I remember the first time I ever saw you. You pushed your way through a crowd of reporters and suddenly I couldn't remember what I was saying. I stared at your shaggy halo and these huge gray eyes and every thought went out of my head. Then you opened your mouth and—very belligerently—asked what in the heck I was doing about unemployment."

He laughed softly. "After that, every time I saw you I could feel your antagonism." He looked at her sternly. "You asked some damned uncomfortable questions, sweet."

"That was my job," she said, shrugging in unconcern, refusing to tell him that the reason she had felt antagonistic was because she had already felt his magic pulling at her and it had terrified her even then.

"Maybe so," he said ruefully, "But you sure got a lot of pleasure out of seeing me squirm. You took a sadistic delight in torturing me."

"Me?" she asked in offended innocence. "Now would I do something like that?" At his vigorous nod, she raised up to grasp his shoulders. "You're the one who is the expert in torture. Flying in and out of my life these last few weeks until I thought I could scream with frustration."

She parted her legs and leaned back, straddling his slim waist. "And now I'm going to pay you back for every minute I suffered," she said, leering evilly. "What do you think of that, Mr. Bigshot Senator?"

He chuckled as her head dipped and she nipped sharply at his neck. "I'm a fair man," he said thoughtfully. "And if you think you deserve revenge, I'm sure I can take anything you can dish out."

"You think so, huh?" She lowered her head to his chest and began nuzzling her way to the hidden male nipples. Her tongue flicked out, teasing them until they felt deliciously taut and suddenly the game took on a deeper meaning.

His sharply indrawn breath and the memory of the ecstasy they had just shared sent her mind and fingers on a different, more urgent course. She slid back, settling her buttocks on his firm thighs as she explored his body with her hands and lips, feeling his strength, tasting the salty skin.

She felt his hardened maleness pressing into the soft flesh of her stomach and moved her body against its heat, sliding lower as her lips roamed into new territory. Her fingers left swirling caresses on and around his stomach and below, then suddenly she grasped the heated shaft, shivering as she heard his erotic cry.

"God!" he rasped out, clutching her shoulders to throw her on her back. "You're driving me mad!"

He loomed above her, spreading her thighs urgently, then thrust deep and hard, his breath coming in harsh, painful gasps. His stormy possession rocked her to her foundations and she met each thrust with frantic eagerness, her fingers sinking deep into the muscles of his strong back.

The violent, shuddering climax left them weak, and it was some time later before Angie had the strength to raise her eyelids. She looked at him and said in a shaky voice, "Well, I guess I showed you."

His soft laugh was just as shaky. "You can show me anytime, Angel." Suddenly he opened his eyes and gazed down at her. "Why is it that I can't get enough of you?" he whispered, his brown eyes holding her still. "What kind of magic do you use on me? All my adult life I've traveled the same course, never quite happy, but content. Then suddenly you appear, rising from the dirt and rubble like phoenix from the ashes, showing me what was missing in my life. I'm just surprised I didn't see it sooner."

"I don't think either of us was too bright," she murmured, laughing softly. "I thought I was dead from the neck down. I had almost decided I was one of those people who just don't need sex." She drew in her breath. "Boy, was I wrong."

"No," he whispered roughly. "You weren't wrong. Because you don't need sex. You need me. And I need you." He lifted her hand and pressed it to his chest. "Can you feel my heart beating? It's beating for you. Don't you understand, Angel? Everything we've ever thought or done or said has been leading up to this."

She stared up at him, her hand making wide circles on his chest as she considered his words. Suddenly she felt threatened. She didn't want to hear the serious note in his voice. She wanted to think about what he had done to her body and not worry about what he was doing to her heart.

"It was meant to be, Angel," he said, lying still as her hand made unconscious, wandering strokes across his body. "It's what we were both born for."

She looked into his eyes and fell deeper under his velvet spell. There was danger here, but somehow she couldn't muster her defenses. She was too deeply entranced to fight the spreading warmth, the delicious weakness. Then suddenly as her caressing hand slid lower, she gasped in surprise.

"Sam," she said in bewilderment, glancing down at his hard, brown body. "Do you have bionic parts you forgot to tell me about? That's not humanly possible, is it?"

"Shall we see?" he said, laughing wickedly as he covered her body with his.

Seven

Angie wrapped the short terry robe around her naked body as she tiptoed stealthily through the living room. Reaching the kitchen door she glanced back over her shoulder in a furtive movement, then when the door swung shut behind her, sighed in relief and walked quickly to the refrigerator to pull out a paper carton. She grabbed a handful of chocolate chip cookies from a ceramic frog with one hand, while pouring a tall glass of milk with the other.

After greedily stuffing a cookie into her mouth, she lifted the glass to her lips and gulped down the divine liquid. Shifting her position, she leaned her hip against the cabinet and smiled with satisfaction, then swung around guiltily when she heard the slap of bare feet on the kitchen floor behind her.

"Sam!" she gasped, wiping the white mustache from her upper lip. Clasping the glass in both hands, she hugged it to her chest protectively and backed away from him, her eyes widening as they ran irresistibly over his firm, brown body. "Now Sam," she said, holding up one hand to ward him off as she stared warily at the gleam in his eyes. "I need food."

When he kept walking steadily in her direction, his teeth bared in a wolfish grin, she backed against the wall and pointed to the clock. "For heaven's sake, Sam, it's six o'clock! We've missed breakfast, lunch, and now dinner. If you're trying to starve me into submission, it's working like a charm."

He didn't answer, but merely stepped closer until he was a breath away. He placed his hands flat on the wall, one on either side of her head, preventing any further retreat.

Looking up at him through her lashes, she gave him her most beguiling smile. "Just one small bowl of cereal?"

He leaned down to flick a crumb from her lip with his tongue, then lowered one hand to take the glass she still held cradled against her breasts. After swallowing a small sip, he murmured, his voice soft and sensual, "Now we've had dinner," then his head descended slowly and he began to leisurely devour her swollen, tender lips.

After a hard fought battle that lasted exactly three seconds, Angie cravenly laid down her arms, willingly outwitted by his superior battle tactics. "I need to lose a few pounds anyway," she whispered, molding her body to his with a sigh of pleasure.

He pushed the robe off her shoulders and leaned down to smooth his lips across the soft flesh. "Have you ever made love on a table?" he murmured against the warm skin.

"I can't say that I have, but"—she tilted her head back to give him access to the long line of her neck—"why not? It's the only place we've missed today."

His laugh was a husky, exciting sound as he lowered his body to press the evidence of his desire more firmly against her. "Except the bathtub," he breathed against her neck. "And it's too limiting."

"It is?" The words came out as a distracted sigh, her thoughts taken over entirely by the way his lips roamed down her neck to the tops of her swelling breasts.

"Uh-huh," he murmured. "I can't hold my breath that long."

She sucked in a huge gulp of air and leaned weakly against the wall as his words brought vivid, erotic pictures to her mind, her eyes glazing over with remembered pleasures.

"Lord," he groaned, straightening to stare at her face. "I love it when your eyes get big and crazy like that. It makes me want to think up new ways to love you, just so I can see it."

Then with one urgent but decisive movement he lifted her off her feet. "The table will still be there tomorrow," he murmured hoarsely as he kicked open the kitchen door and carried her down the hall to the bedroom.

Sitting cross-legged in the middle of the bed,

Angie spooned the last bit of cereal and fruit into her mouth, then sighed in repletion and looked up at the man sitting beside her.

"I never thought Post Toasties and bananas could taste so ambrosial," she said. "You're a wonderfully inventive cook, Senator Sam."

"Just one of my many talents." He gave her a surprisingly boyish grin when she nodded in vigorous agreement, then took the bowl from her to place it along with his on the nightstand. Leaning back against the headboard, he caught her eyes and held them with his serious expression. "We need to talk now, sweetheart."

He paused, lifting her hand to caress each long finger in turn before returning his eyes to hers. "I want to get married, Angel."

She jerked her hand away as though he had held a match to it. "Married? To me?" she asked, her face stiff with shock.

"No, to Bette Midler," he said drily. "Of course, to you. I can't believe it hasn't occurred to you too. Just think about what's been happening between us." His voice suddenly took on an urgent excitement. "Angel, I know you don't have a lot to compare it with, but, sweetheart, what we have together is something unique. And I'm not just talking about what happens when we make love—although that in itself is pretty mind-boggling. I mean the way we click in everything. When we're together something special—something real happens."

He stared for a moment at her shocked, confused face, then continued, his voice low and husky. "I love you, Angel. I don't want you temporarily. I need forever to be a part of our relationship."

His hand was sliding up her arm, sending shivers of need trembling to the heart of her. His voice played its magic on her ears, causing her to lean involuntarily in his direction. He loved her. The incredible words sang in her blood and champagne bubbles burst in her head.

Jumping off the bed, she gasped, "Wait . . . stop," speaking more to her soaring emotions than to Sam. She glanced back at him, then away hurriedly, chewing on the inside of her jaw as she tried to assimilate her thoughts.

"You're right. We need to talk." She twisted her hands together nervously. "First of all I want you to know that what you said"—she hesitated, then closed her eyes in determination and continued—"about loving me. That's the most beautiful thing that's ever happened to me. And I'll—I'll treasure the memory, Sam."

She opened her eyes wide and swung around when she heard his violently muttered curse. "Wait. I know that sounds like a kiss-off, but I mean it."

His eyes were closed, his head tilted back, exposing the taut muscles of his neck. She studied his blank expression, then tried again. "Forget about that right now. Let me tell you some things about me, Sam. Then maybe you'll understand."

She sat down on the edge of the bed. "Something happened to me when I was a kid. I can't tell you when it happened or why it happened or even what it was exactly that happened. I only know that by the time I was a teenager, I felt I was fighting a war. A war inside me. There is something in my make-up—I don't know, maybe I was born with it—that *wants* me to fail." She sighed shakily. "I told you my mother wanted me to be

Miss Popularity. Well, it wasn't that I didn't want all those girl things for myself; it was simply that I *couldn't* be those things. I used my writing as an excuse for my failure. Then later I told myself I couldn't get anywhere as a reporter because I was stuck in a small town, but it was years before I forced myself to leave."

She stood in agitation. "Now I'm in the same situation again. I've been using my hypersensitive nature as a reason for my failure here. But the simple truth is this thing inside me was working again, willing me to destroy everything I've worked for."

When she raised her head to look at him, she found his sharp eyes trained intently on her face. "Sam," she said softly, "this is my last chance. If I screw up again, I might as well give up. I've already wasted too many years."

She gave a broken, mocking laugh. "It would be so easy to say to hell with my career and marry you. Because you're right. There is something special between us. When you hold me I forget everything. But neither of us would ever know if I did it because I love you or because I was willing myself to fail again."

Placing a hand under her chin, he raised her eyes to meet his. "Why does it have to be an either-or proposition, Angel? Why can't you marry me and continue with your career?"

She stared at him as though he had lost his mind. "You're kidding," she said in disbelief. "Think about it a minute. Even if I didn't work as a reporter, I'll always be a writer. Good, bad, or indifferent—I have to be. It's a part of me. And how could I be an honest writer if I were always worried about how my work would affect your career? Sam, try to remember the political wives who have publicly expressed their opinions in the last few years. Where are their husbands now? They were ushered into obscurity by their outspoken wives." She shook her head. "You're presidential material and we both know it. Now wouldn't I just make one humdinger of a First Lady?"

"Yes," he said stubbornly. "You would—that's always supposing I wanted the presidency in the first place and that I was elected in the second. And if it's meant to be, then your being honest won't stop it."

"You're being deliberately hard-headed and just plain dumb," she said in exasperation. "The first time I opened my mouth, they would crucify you."

"You want to know what's dumb?" he said, jerking her closer with an angry movement. "Dumb is letting something go that I've been looking for all my life." His voice softened and he threaded tense fingers through her hair. "Dumb is being without you, Angel."

Her lip quivered uncontrollably, but she looked him squarely in the eye as she said, "A man who holds the public trust has to have a wife who sinks graciously into the background. Any woman who loved you would be glad to do that for you, Sam." She drew in a deep breath. "So I guess I don't, because I don't think I could ever change that much."

He held himself tight and stiff for a moment, closing his eyes as he hugged her fiercely close. She could almost feel the pain in him and it hurt more deeply than anything she had ever felt.

There was a sheen of supressed tears in her

eyes when he pulled her head away from his chest and looked down at her. "I guess that's that then," he said wryly, then astonishingly his brown eyes began to twinkle. "You wanna have an affair instead?"

She buried her face in his neck, the tears escaping as she laughed weakly. "Oh God, Sam, I'd love to have an affair with you."

"Good," he said, giving her a quick, remarkably carefree kiss before getting up to go into the bathroom. He turned on the shower, then called back to her where she sat, open-mouthed, on the bed. "We'll start the thing officially tomorrow. At my ranch outside Austin."

She walked to the bathroom door and watched as he stepped under the water. "Officially?"

"Right." When she walked closer, he reached out and pulled her in with him. "Today is completely off the record."

The stream of warm water caught her off guard and she laughed in surprise, hiding her face against his chest. "I've never had an official affair before," she said, licking a trail of water from his shoulder. "Come to think of it, I've never had an unofficial one either. The only thing I've ever had was an uncategorized mistake."

"Wrong again, O Befuddled One." He moved her slick body against his. "We're having our unofficial affair today."

"By golly, I believe you're right," she said, glancing down at the hardened shaft pressing against her. Her eyelids began to drift down weakly, then she looked up at him, struck by a sudden thought. "Lord, I bet you were something when you were eighteen."

"I beg your pardon. I believe I'm something now."

"That's what I mean," she said, laughing at the offended look on his face. "A man's sexual peak is supposed to be at age eighteen. If you're on the decline now, I would have died of starvation at your peak." Her eyes grew big and glazed. "The mind boggles at the thought."

He picked up the soap and lathered his hands, then said softly, "I don't care what the experts say. A man's sexual peak is when he meets the woman he loves." His soapy hands began to make swirls on her shoulders and down her arms. "And for me, that's now."

Angie leaned against the wall, weak with pleasure, as his nimble fingers caught her breasts, soaping and massaging them, his thumbs circling the peaks until they stood out tight and pebble hard. A slow, consuming fire spread as he worked his way down her ribs, across her stomach to soap and probe the curling triangle of hair between her thighs, then—devilishly—moved on to her thighs and the soft backs of her knees.

He stood slowly, moving his body up hers, then turned her around to lean back against him and assisted the water in removing the soap from her body. Every stroke of his hand sent her deeper under his now familiar spell and she knew suddenly that this was the most powerful thing she had ever come up against. So powerful, in fact, that she very much doubted she would ever be able to fight it.

Then all thoughts of fighting fled when he leaned her back against the wall of the shower and began to sip the water from the places his hands had already sought. He held her full breasts together and moved his mouth from one to the other, sucking the warm water from the nipples, licking it from the rounded flesh.

Her fingers clutched his shoulders when his mouth slid down her ribs, pausing to tease the moisture from her navel before dipping lower. "Sam," she gasped. "I thought you said making love in the bathtub was too limiting."

"That's only if you're taking a bath," he murmured against the inside of her thigh. "A shower is different." A tormenting flick of his tongue sent a fiery shaft of ecstasy searing through her and she whimpered helplessly as the exquisite agony drained her of her strength.

"You see," he said, his voice suddenly near her ear. "Anything's possible in the shower." He leaned down to grasp her buttocks in both hands. "Hold on to me, sweet, and I'll show you."

He lifted her and, as she locked her legs around his waist, slowly filled her. The pleasure, the sweet torture, left her powerless to do anything other than clutch his shoulders and ride out the storm that built immeasurably under the massaging stream of warm water. She heard him cry out his fulfillment and tighten his grip on her buttocks in an incredibly erotic movement, moments before she felt the explosive burst of spiraling electric sensations, then a sweet, thick warmth flooded her body and her head sagged weakly against his shoulder.

Please, she thought desperately, moving her mouth languidly against his neck, listening as his breathing returned to normal, please don't let him ask anything of me now. Because if he asked me to die for him right now, I'd do it willingly and laugh for pure joy as I did.

"Angel?" he said in a husky whisper, pulling her face away from his neck so he could see her face. "Angel, you're crying!"

"I know," she said, laughing and crying at the same time as her feet slid down to touch the bottom of the tub. "Beauty affects me that way. I cry when I see a sunset, too."

For a moment his face was strange and stunned and vulnerable, then he raised her hand to gently kiss her palm. "Thank you," was all he said as he smoothed the damp hair away from her face, but his eyes told her so much more.

He was so many things, this man who loved her. He was gentle and strong. Loving and giving. Honest and true. Vulnerable and fierce. And he would never know that it was all these things that finally and irrevocably convinced her that she was wrong for him. For some strange reason, trying to live up to such a man—such a love—scared the hell out of her.

She hid her sad smile as he helped her from the tub and wrapped a bath towel around her.

"Come to bed," he said, grabbing the ends of the towel to pull her closer. "I want to tell you about my home."

As they snuggled together under the cover, she asked, "I thought you had an apartment here in Dallas."

"I do. And one in D.C. But my home is just outside Austin." He locked his hands behind his head on the pillow. "You'll love it, Angel. When you get there it will have everything a man could possibly want."

She reached out to tease the curling hair on his chest. "Sam, why did we suddenly decide to go to Austin?" she asked lazily.

"Because here I can see 'senator' in your eyes too often. At the ranch I hope you'll be able to see just Sam—or maybe even Cowboy Sam, but whatever you see will be closer to the truth than what you see here."

"Cowboy Sam," she said slowly, then sat up and looked down at him. "You said it's a ranch?"

"Yes, why?" he asked, turning his head to look at her quizzically.

"I suppose you have animals—horses and cows and things—on this ranch?"

"Angel," he said, hiding his smile. "There aren't too many petunia ranches in this part of the country."

She leaned her elbows on her bent knees, tugging at her ear thoughtfully. "I grew up in a small town. A small *Texas* town. But, Sam, I've never been within ten feet of a horse in my life. And cows!" She turned her head to look at him indignantly. "If they're so placid and amiable, why do they all have horns? The only livestock I've been intimately acquainted with were chickens—and they chased me up a tree! I swear they were Alfred Hitchcock rejects."

She rose to her knees, her face wary. "Sam," she whispered. "Animals don't like me. Even gerbils bare their teeth when I walk by. Couldn't we go to Idaho and let me see you as Farmer Sam, instead?"

He pulled her down to his chest, his laughter filling the bedroom. "Trust me, love," he chuckled.

"Once you get used to them, you'll see there's nothing to be afraid of."

"You I trust," she muttered. "Animals are a different can of beans."

For a moment she lay there, silently listening to his soft laughter. then she ran her hand up the strong cords in his neck and said quietly, "You haven't given up the idea of marriage, have you?"

"I'm not a quitter, Angel," he said slowly. "And although I know you think your reasons are valid ones, I'll never believe there isn't some way to work it out." He looked down at her, his eyes burning with conviction. Then he leaned his head back and smiled. "But I want you to put all that out of your mind for right now. For the next week I want you simply to relax and have fun."

Eight

"Sam?"

Angie clenched her teeth as her bottom met the saddle forcefully. "Sam, am I having fun?"

"You're doing fine," he said, grinning. "I told you you're a natural."

"A natural," she muttered, grunting as she once again collided with hard leather. "Isn't that what they used to call the village idiot?"

Looking up at him wryly, she was struck once again by the difference in him. With the sun shining down on his tanned face, the hat resting casually on his brown hair, the plain cotton shirt and sturdy levis, it was difficult to believe he had ever worn anything as sophisticated as a suit and tie. This new look seemed natural to him. As did the beautiful ranch house that had stolen her heart at first sight. Its white walls and high green roof had at first seemed too plain, too homey to be a part of the famous senator, but soon, as he had predicted, Washington and the world of politics had faded from her thoughts, leaving only the man who sat beside her on the porch every evening, softly whistling old-fashioned love songs as they watched the sun go down.

The beautiful, green valley that held his home had begun seducing her from the moment she arrived four days earlier. It contained peace and beauty. And it contained Sam. In a way it seemed she had been there only a short time, but then again everything felt so familiar, as though she had always been there.

The couple Sam trusted to care for his home—a Mexican-American housekeeper with the unlikely name of Bridget and her taciturn husband, Frank—had accepted Angie as part of their family without hesitation. Which, of course, made Angie wonder how often Sam brought home strange women on the spur of the moment.

At her insistence it had been Frank who had introduced her to horses. Sam had wanted the honor, but she told him that if she were going to make a fool of herself, she would do it without his assistance. So he had disappeared for hours that first morning while Angie had become intimately acquainted with a horse, and the dusty ground in the corral, and—on one occasion—the small, cold stream that ran behind the house.

Her hard-headedness saved her that day. She eventually decided that even though it was a close race she was smarter than a horse, and she refused to be outwitted by any animal called Snookums.

Every time she landed on her rear she picked herself up, saluted a gleefully watching Bridget, and limped back to the horse. Frank would shake his head, spit a stream of tobacco juice in the dirt, then help her back on. And by early afternoon she had managed to circumnavigate the house and barn without slipping sideways more than five or six times.

Although her head was hard, Angie had discovered her bottom wasn't. When she had greeted Sam that afternoon with a hearty, "Howdy, pardner," he hadn't been fooled for a minute and had even had the nerve to laugh when she told him she preferred to eat standing up because as a child she had been frightened by a chair.

She grinned up at him now, remembering that night in his bed. She knew now how he had advanced so quickly in his chosen field. The man was a genius at improvisation.

Suddenly he reached across to drag her from her horse, settling her before him on his own saddle. "It seems to me that I recall a little known Texas statute that prohibits being provocative while on a horse."

"Yuh caught me red-handed, Sheriff. So what are yuh goin' to do about it?" she drawled, then, "Sam! What are you doing?" as he began to unbutton her plaid shirt.

"You look hot," he said innocently, lifting one rounded breast free of her lacy bra.

"And you really think this will cool me down?"

"I know a place, Angel," he murmured as he dipped his head to trace the impudent nipple with his tongue. "It's not far from here. The grass is soft and cool and emerald green, the branches of a willow tree dip down to trail its leaves in a tiny stream—and under that willow you're surrounded by a spring green curtain that lets in just enough sunlight to make it a magic place."

He lifted his head in time to catch her sigh with his lips. Moments later, she murmured languidly against his neck, "You told Bridget we would be back in time for lunch."

"Did I?" His breath was warm and seductive against her forehead. "Do you suppose she believed me?"

She chuckled. "She said if you were late you would have to cook your own dinner tonight."

He sighed. "She did, didn't she." Lifting Angie's chin, he ran his thumb across her lower lip. "After lunch?" he murmured huskily.

"After lunch," she agreed softly.

When he lifted her back onto her horse she slid sideways precariously. Leaning forward urgently, she hugged Snookums' scruffy neck, shifted her position carefully until she was once more sitting upright, then smiled happily at Sam. "By golly, I'm getting to be a regular Annie Oakley. I can even tell when Snookums—Lord, what a name—is going to try to bite me."

"Come on, Annie," he laughed, casting her a look that took her completely by surprise. The look held amusement and a kind of deep content, but what drew her up short was the pride she glimpsed in his eyes.

As she stared, his expression changed and—after thinking over the way she stayed on her horse, more from sheer blind luck than any real skill— she decided she had been mistaken. Turning her horse in a wide circle, she followed him home.

They managed to make it back with a few seconds to spare and, after cleaning up, Angie once again tried to wade through a meal that would have balked the Pittsburgh Steelers. Lunch to her had always meant a salad or sandwich, and in the four days she had been exposed to Bridget's cooking she still wasn't used to what the housekeeper called "a bite to eat." Chicken fried steak, cream gravy, mashed potatoes, corn on the cob, sliced tomatoes, wedges of cantaloupe, followed by strawberries drowned in thick, fresh cream sat clustered together on a table Angie could have sworn was sagging in the middle.

"Bridget," she said, her eyes widening as the petite woman added fresh green beans to the table. "It all looks . . . wonderful."

Sam sat down, hiding his grin. He knew how much trouble Angie had getting through lunch. But he also knew that she wouldn't risk hurting Bridget's feelings by refusing to eat what was offered.

Bridget was an exquisite cook and she was proud of the fact. Although she ate like a bird herself, she expected everyone else to eat like Sam and Frank. Angie had tried early in the week to explain that although she enjoyed her food, there was a limit to what the human body could take in. The explanation had completely missed its mark. Bridget assumed if anyone didn't eat her cooking it was because she had failed to make it attractive enough.

She took Angie's plate and began to fill it, smiling widely. "Thank you, Miz Angel. You haven't had a chance to try my cream gravy yet. Frank swears I wouldn't have to cook any meat long as I put enough of this gravy on the table."

"If you cooked it, I know it will be delicious," Angie replied, swallowing hard as Bridget continued to ladle food onto the plate.

Sam wasn't even trying to hide the laughter in his eyes and, as Bridget turned away to get homemade rolls, Angie quickly picked up her plate, shoveled some of the food onto Sam's, then lifted her fork to her lips just as Bridget turned around.

Thereafter, every time the housekeeper turned her back, Angie disposed of more of her food and at the end of the meal watched with innocent eyes from behind a clean plate as Bridget scolded Sam for not eating enough.

"You fiend," Sam said as they left the house. "I can hardly breath. It's a good thing we have to walk half a mile to the stream."

They walked the half mile quickly, following a narrow, rocky trail through cedars and scrub oak, then suddenly the trail ended and they stepped into another world.

"It's beautiful," she breathed in awe as she gazed around her. The willow tree that dominated the small clearing was just as he had described it and below a bend in the stream was a pebble-lined pool filled with crystal clear water.

He pulled her down with him to sit on the cool, green carpet of grass. "When I was a boy and came to stay with my grandparents, this is where I always ended up. I would lie here counting clouds and dreaming of you."

"You didn't know me when you were a boy," she reminded him softly.

"That's a technicality. Anyway, if I had known

you, this is where I would have dreamed about you." He picked up a small stone and threw it into the pool, watching as the circular ripples grew and spread over the small surface. "And that's where I went skinny dipping."

"Skinny dipping?" she asked, her imagination running wild as she examined his hard frame.

"Uh-huh," he said slowly, a matching gleam in his eyes as his gaze drifted down her body. "Skinny dipping."

Their thoughts in perfect accord, they jumped up and with eager fingers discarded their clothing. After the first icy shock, their bodies adjusted quickly to the water in the spring-fed pool and they played and splashed like children, sliding together frequently beneath the clear water, pausing occasionally to warm themselves lazily in the late afternoon sun.

And when he carried her beneath the willow tree and lay down with her behind the spring green curtain, their lovemaking seemed a natural extension of the simplicity of the day. It contained no artifice, no reminders of the hectic world in which they lived. It was basic and innocent. It was pure pagan pleasure.

Lying on her stomach afterward, Angie rested her head on her crossed arms and stared at his sleeping face. It had taken her a long time to admit it to herself, but today had been too honest for her to deceive herself any longer. She loved him, and probably had even as she searched for him in the cave. The feelings that had confused her then had grown stronger every day, until now she was fairly bursting with them. And for today she wasn't going to think of the consequences of loving him. The loving was enough for today. Maybe Sam was right. Maybe there was a way to work it out, she thought as her eyelids drifted down. There had to be a way. . . .

When they awoke, the afternoon sun hung low over the hills. They silently helped each other dress and slowly walked back to the house, each unknowingly trying to prolong the wonder of the day.

But inevitably they reached the house and the world they were trying to avoid caught up with them quicker than they had expected.

"Congressman Pendergast called, Mr. Sam," Bridget said as they walked in the door. "He says can you pick him and Miz Pendergast up at the airport and he'll go with you to the fund-raisin' ball tomorrow and then fly back to Houston with his brother."

"Damnation!"

The vehemence of Sam's muttered curse surprised Angie. When Bridget left the room, she put her arms around his waist and looked up at his frowning face. "What's wrong, Sam? I thought Jim Pendergast was a friend of yours from way back."

"He is," he said, running his fingers through his hair in distraction. "I just wish he had picked another time to drop in on me. Of all people . . ." He sounded exasperated and worried. "Look, Angel, when they get here, don't make any judgments—don't think at all until I talk to you."

"What are you talking about?" He had her completely baffled.

"I haven't got time to explain now." He grabbed her, pulling her close to give her a fierce, breath-stealing kiss. "Just remember that you are you and I am me and nothing anyone else does has anything to do with us." With those cryptic words, he left as she stared after him in puzzled silence.

Minutes later as she stepped into the bathtub she began going over his words, but she could make no kind of sense of them. She had forgotten all about the fund-raising ball he had told her would take place in the capital on Saturday night—tomorrow. It seemed as though the world was pushing in on them with a vengeance. The problems she had decided they could solve after a while wouldn't be put off much longer.

When she thought about that later in the evening, she almost laughed at the irony. Not only would the problems not be put off, they came up and slapped her in the face that night.

When she first met Louise Pendergast she thought she was an exceptionally shy woman to have such a public husband. Then as Angie began to watch her closely, she sensed that it was something more than mere shyness.

It wasn't until after dinner that the situation became clear and she knew why Sam had acted so strangely.

She caught his sharp eye on her as he stood beside his friend by the window in the living room, then turned to the woman sitting beside her on the couch.

"Do you enjoy living in Washington, Louise?"

The thin, raven-haired woman glanced nervously toward her husband, then down at her hands twisted together in her lap, then back to Angie. "It's . . . um . . . a wonderful place."

Angie's eyes narrowed. "And your home in Houston? Do you enjoy getting back to it?"

Again the nervous glance. "Jim says . . . Houston is the only place to live outside Washington."

All evening Angie had listened as the Congressman's wife had carefully avoided giving a direct answer. If she were in her husband's company, she would defer to him. If she were not, she would get a hunted look in her eyes and preface her sentence with "Jim says."

"I believe Sam said you have children?"

Ah, here was a question she could answer. Angie watched the relief spread across her face as she spoke.

"Yes," she sighed gratefully. "Yes, we do."

"How many?" That one surely couldn't be too tough.

"Three."

Good Lord! It was like pulling teeth. Angie supressed the urge to shake the poor woman and tried again. "Do you work outside the home?"

Her eyes darted around the room feverishly and suddenly Angie felt as though she were dealing out some kind of subtle torture, as though she were slowly pulling the wings off a butterfly. No, not a butterfly. A nervous little gypsy moth.

"I . . . well . . ." Louise stammered. "I don't know if you would call it—"

"What is it that you do, Louise?" Angie asked softly, her eyes now sharing the woman's pain.

"Louise and you have something in common, Angela."

Congressman Pendergast had come silently to

stand beside the couch. He smiled encouragingly at his wife as he continued. "She's something of a writer, too."

"Really?" Angie said, trying to hide her surprise.

"No—no, not really," Louise protested.

"Sure you are, honey. Why don't you tell Angela about it?"

He moved away to refill his drink and left a huge silence behind him.

"Would you like to tell me about your work, Louise? You don't have to talk about it if you don't want to."

"No, of course I don't mind talking about it," she said, her voice sounding overeager as though she were afraid she had offended Angie. "It's just that it's nothing really. I do a regular feature in a local magazine—that is, a Texas magazine. I describe the furnishings in a different home each month." Her voice began to trail away. "Someone else does the photographs," she murmured apologetically.

The men joined them then, bringing a sigh of relief from both Angie and Louise, and they eagerly turned the conversation over to them.

When they finally parted company an hour later, Angie walked silently to Sam's bedroom. Closing the door behind them, Sam leaned against it and watched as she began removing her clothes.

"She drinks on the sly, too," he said quietly.

Turning around to face him, she sent him a questioning glance.

"Louise," he explained. "I thought you might as well have all the facts so we could get it out in the open."

"Get it out in the open?"

"You know what I'm talking about," he said, pushing away from the door. "I knew this would happen, but there was nothing I could do to stop it. I saw you watching her, analyzing her. And it sure didn't take long for the panic to start showing in your eyes, did it? All the progress we've made this week, wiped out in a few minutes."

He sat wearily on the bed, his elbows resting on his thighs, his hands clasped loosely between his knees. "I asked you not to make any judgments until I could talk to you."

"And what would you have said?" she asked tightly. "What could you have added to what I saw tonight?"

"I could have said she's not you," he said softly. "I could have said she would be exactly the way she is even if Jim were a hot dog vendor."

"You don't really believe that," she said, feeling drained.

"Okay," he admitted with a heavy sigh. "Maybe that's an exaggeration. But Angel, Louise has problems. Personality problems. Any stress—political or otherwise—would have affected her in the same way."

"I have problems, too!" Angie said in a strained whisper. She wanted to shout the words, but couldn't take a chance on disturbing Sam's guests.

"You're a fighter, Angel," he said, standing to pull her into his arms. "You would never give way to the pressure the way Louise has." He paused, then said urgently, "It will be different for us."

Later she lay beside him in bed, her body still warm from the loving, her nostrils still filled with the scent of him. As her wide-open eyes stared sightlessly at the ceiling, she listened to his quiet breathing while his words echoed silently in her brain.

"You would never give way to the pressure." Perhaps he was right. Perhaps she wouldn't let the pressure drive her quietly insane as Louise had, but that didn't mean the pressure wouldn't be just as strong.

All the restrictions—some admittedly self-imposed—that applied to Louise because of her husband's profession would apply to Angie as well. And the fact that she wouldn't break under the pressure wouldn't make it any less felt. It would only mean that she would remain sane while she held her tongue and squelched her instincts—and somehow she felt that a little bit of insanity could only help such a dreary future.

Now that she had admitted to herself that she loved Sam, her choice should have been easier. But it wasn't. She wasn't naïve enough to believe that because two people love each other their happiness is guaranteed. If she tried to fit the mold of the good political wife, she would lose respect for herself and would probably grow to resent Sam. And if she didn't try to change—this was the thought that terrified—if she didn't, he would come to resent her. She had been around the political arena long enough to know you either played the game or you got lost in the shuffle.

Okay, smart stuff, she thought miserably, so now you know you've been fooling yourself this week. But how are you going to convince Sam of that?

If there were only some way to show him that public opinion would be against her when she acted naturally, without guarding her tongue. She could start with the Pendergasts, but they were personal friends and would most likely hide their reactions.

Where their relationship was concerned, Sam was like a mule. She would have to hit him on the head with a two-by-four first just to get his attention. She would need something extremely public.

The fund-raising ball. For a moment she scared herself with the idea, then she knew she had hit on the very thing to make an impression. All the party celebrities would be there. All she had to do was circulate and give honest opinions. His associates would do the rest. They were on Sam's side and would be prompt in letting him know that she had to be gotten rid of—for the good of the party.

Nine

Angie took a sip of her champagne and glanced again around the huge ballroom that was the show-piece of the restored mansion on the outskirts of Austin.

Someone must have forgotten to tell them that Ziegfeld is dead, she thought drily, taking in the elaborate, glittering decorations and ball gowns. As her eyes came full circle and clashed with Sam's, she drew in her breath sharply.

That look was in his eyes again. She hoped it wasn't as obvious to everyone else as it was to her, but she was very much afraid it was.

She had seen it first when she had walked into the living room earlier that night to join Sam and the Pendergasts. It had begun as a spark of admiration as he took in the silver-blond hair piled high on her head in careless curls. Then when his eyes drifted down over the slim white satin gown, draped low in the front and to the waist in the back, the gleam had turned into a brightly blazing fire.

And apparently the fire hadn't died down. She turned her flushed face away from his steady gaze. When she had first seen the look in his eyes, she had had to fight an impulse to drop the whole thing. Now she lifted her chin in determination. She had already danced with both Sam and Jim. It was time. She turned around and began to search the room for a likely candidate.

Her eyes passed over a group of people to her left, then returned swiftly. If she was not mistaken, at the center of the group was Harrison Turner, the party's national chairman.

"Introduce me," she murmured to Sam, avoiding his eyes as she moved in that direction.

After the introductions, a wary-eyed Sam was cornered by a large woman who looked like a cross between Caligula and Mae West, and Angie took the opportunity to move in for the kill.

"Mr. Turner," she said sweetly. "You're always so well informed in your interviews—maybe you can tell me something about the new bill a member of your party is sponsoring now. Do you really think it will be effective in clearing the major waterways of pollution?"

"Well, Miss—Jones, was it?" At her nod, he continued. "Miss Jones, I have every confidence that once passed the bill will be just what we're looking for in America today. I'm not saying compromises won't be made. That's part of the game. But when we get it rolling, I'm sure you'll agree that it's the best proposal we've come across yet."

All of which told her just exactly nothing. "I understand it will take time, but nothing's being done in the meantime."

"Not true. No," he said, smiling broadly, "I think if you'll go back and check your facts, you'll find that at every—hard core, shall we say—pollution point, we have experts on the site, working full time on finding solutions to these problems."

"But what are they doing?" she persisted.

"Why, if you could see all the reports that come in every day—the same reports, by the way, that were used in forming this new bill—you wouldn't have to ask that question."

She stared at him silently for a moment, then said, "Have you shown the reports to the fish?"

"I—" He started to answer, then her question sank in and he stopped short. His eyes narrowed and she could see he was reevaluating her, but before he could form an answer, someone called his name. As he turned away, he murmured kindly, "Maybe Sam could explain it to you better."

She stared at his back, wondering just what Sam was supposed to explain to her.

"I heard what you were saying, little lady, and let me tell you, I agree one hundred percent."

Angie turned to face the flamboyantly dressed man who had spoken. It took her a moment to place him, but when she did, she realized she had caught an even bigger fish. The man standing before her so confidently was one of the wealthiest men in Texas and could always be counted on for hefty contributions. No wonder he was so confident. He was used to being courted by the most important men in the country.

"You agree, Mr. Seitz?" she murmured.

"Damn right, I do, honey. And I've been telling 'em—if you want ol' Andy here to come through with the cash, y'all better stop pussyfootin' around and shut off some of them plants that are ruinin' this country."

"So you blame big business for the continuing pollution?"

"Why sure," he said in surprise. "Them and the government that's been lettin' them get away with it."

"Wrong," she said sweetly.

He stared for a moment at her smile as though fascinated, then her words seemed to penetrate and his eyes widened. "Wrong? Then who is?"

"It's not the government and it's not big business. It's you, Mr. Seitz."

"Me!" he said indignantly. "I don't have anything to do with that. I'm in real estate."

She hid her smile as his lazy drawl disappeared. "What do you think those plants are manufacturing? And who are they producing goods for?"

"Well . . ." he blustered, beginning to get a hunted look. "How should I know?"

"That's just the point. If you're so concerned, you should make it your business to know." She paused, giving him a chance to wipe his brow with his handkerchief. "We Americans have come to include the most ridiculous things on our list of necessities. As long as we have to have paper towels and antiperspirant and bug spray, the companies will produce those things. But have you ever looked into the manufacturing process of any of the thousands of products we use every day? No, of course not. No one does. And as long as we keep buying, they'll keep making."

"But it's the government's duty to regulate those things," he said nervously, giving it one last try.

"Look at the position the government's in, Mr. Seitz—may I call you Andy?" At his dazed nod, she continued. "Well, Andy, on one hand you have a relatively small group of actively concerned citizens who represent a few thousand dollars in taxes and on the other hand you have big business representing millions in taxes and who also generate jobs for those concerned citizens. Now, as a smart businessman, who are you going to listen to? Who are you going to work hardest for? Someone once said 'Money doesn't just talk, it screams obscenities.' That may be an uncomfortable fact, but it's a fact nevertheless. And if we ever want to accomplish anything we have to deal in realities.

"The government has a very expensive country to run," she continued. "So what it comes down to is the fact that each individual has to stop it on his own and not look exclusively to the government for the solutions. Which means that you, Andy, are just as responsible for pollution as they are," she finished quietly, and Mr. Seitz was down for the count. She heard him breathe a noisy sigh of relief as she turned away to look for Sam.

She didn't have to search long. Although he was still held by the woman who had taken him captive earlier, his eyes were trained on Angie. She tried for a moment to read his reaction in his face, but to no avail. He was close enough to have heard every word, but he was giving no clue to his feelings.

After her conversation with Mr. Seitz, Angie was pursued actively by people who had a favorite soap box. At first it was enjoyable—she would never find a bigger crowd who was interested in her every word. But soon she came to feel she was an oddity. That she was some kind of performing bear. Yet she didn't let the uncomfortable feeling stop her, and every time she gave an opinion that was in direct opposition to Sam's, her gaze would drift irresistibly back to him.

The only time she saw any kind of emotion on his blank face was during her discussion with a small, motherly woman.

The woman had approached her with an eager look on her pink face and with no introduction or preamble had said, "What about the draft?"

Angie's immediate reaction was to say, "Yes, it is a little windy in here, isn't it?" but she stifled it along with the accompanying giggle and listened quietly as the woman talked on and on about how she was not going to let her daughter fight in any war.

"Do you love your sons less than your daughter?" Angie asked at last.

"I beg your pardon?" The woman stopped her breathless flow of words as she heard Angie's question.

"Do you want your sons to fight wars?"

"No, of course not. But if it's necessary, then it should be the men who fight. Women aren't psychologically suited for it."

"And men are? Are they born killers? I don't think any human is psychologically suited for war. Male or female—we all do what we have to do. And there are sensitive men as well as sensitive women." She paused. She didn't want to come on too strong with this woman. Campaign or no campaign, this was the kind of person who would never really understand and would be very upset if her values became confused.

"Women have been fighting beside their men throughout history," she said softly. "This is only my personal feeling, but if it were really necessary to defend this country, I would rather be out there protecting it than sitting at home, twiddling my thumbs and wondering if my man were being killed." She smiled down at the woman. "What we've got to do is not worry about who's fighting our wars, but about preventing them in the first place."

When Angie turned away, she found herself facing Sam. He didn't speak. He didn't have to—his eyes were eloquent. He merely took her hand, walked her out onto the floor, and took her in his arms.

As they danced the silence continued, but she felt a warmth surrounding her, sinking in through the pores, permeating her vulnerable flesh. She was being seduced by his nearness and suddenly she wanted to leave this gilt-coated world and run back to his green valley. Why did there have to be so many complications? Why couldn't they simply love?

Mentally pulling up short, she realized she was slipping back into the dream that had dominated the past week. And she had already fought that battle once, she couldn't do it again. She had to practice what she preached and deal in realities.

When the dance ended, she pulled away from him and glanced urgently around the room for another victim before she weakened again.

•   •   •

"The 'quality of life' by whose standards?" Angie asked belligerently. All evening she had remained calm, stating her views dispassionately. Now she was mad.

This—this person had ambushed her while she stood alone in the small, enclosed side garden, searching for a breath of the cool, night air. The woman had walked up to her—so confident—and had begun giving her opinions about how the world should be run. That in itself was not unusual. It had happened over and over again tonight. But these types always defeated Angie, driving her wild with frustration. No amount of logic could convince them that they were wrong, simply because they themselves didn't believe in what they were saying. They didn't believe in anything, but considered it chic to have opinions.

She forced herself to speak quietly as she stared at the tall, blonde woman standing with her beside the low wall that surrounded a small lily pond. "Suppose someone told you that because blondes lead such miserable lives, they would be better off dead?"

"That's ridiculous," the woman replied airily. "We don't."

"Ah, but suppose someone told you that you aren't capable of knowing whether or not your life is miserable. Suppose someone decided that blondes have no emotions and simply don't have the capacity to love life. Suppose someone told you that since you aren't a redhead, your life is not valued as highly."

For a moment, the tall woman's eyes blazed with fury. "But that's not fair," she breathed hotly, then her eyes narrowed and she turned to walk away.

Angie caught her arm, forcing the woman to pause. "Exactly," she said quietly.

The woman raised her chin haughtily and said the deathless words, "Turn blue," then pushed backward against Angie to free her arm.

The events that took place next happened so fast, Angie was never sure exactly what went wrong. It could have been that her flimsy evening sandals caught in a crack between the stones of the terrace. Or it could have been the force of the woman's shove. Whatever the cause, the next thing she knew she was sitting in the lily pond, the sun-warmed water reaching up to her ribs.

The splash caused by her fall dampened several of her carefully arranged curls and they hung limply on her forehead. Reaching up to brush them back she sighed in resignation, leaned back against the low stone wall, and raised her eyes to the star-studded heavens. "You're doing this because I'm such a smart ass, right?"

This is not exactly what I had in mind when I decided to start people talking about me tonight, she thought, dipping her fingers nonchalantly into the water. But if she had wanted to cause a stir, this would certainly do it.

A sudden breeze caused goose flesh to appear on her bare arms and she pressed her hands to the bottom of the pool to support herself as she began to stand up, then squeezed her eyes shut in panic when she heard the sharp tap of footsteps on the flagstone terrace.

The footsteps stopped abruptly, then continued more slowly until they reached the small pool.

Angie slowly turned her head to glance over her shoulder. She lifted her gaze from the trousers of a beautifully tailored tuxedo up the white silk shirt to Sam's face.

"Hello," she said casually. "Nice party, isn't it?"

His lips twitched uncontrollably, but he held them firmly still as he replied, "Yes, nice—but it did get a little warm inside. I see you managed to . . . cool off."

If he laughs, she thought almost with disinterest, I'll hit him with a lily pad.

Suddenly he moved and she heard a small splash, then he was standing beside her in his beautiful tuxedo, the water reaching almost to his knees.

"Sam! What on earth do you think you're doing?" she gasped, moving urgently to stand up.

He reached down to lift her into his arms. "I've always been a firm believer in togetherness." He had removed his jacket before joining her and after stepping back over the low wall, he stood her on her feet just long enough to drape it around her shoulders, then picked her up again.

"Sam, you're a fool," she said, laughing helplessly as her head rested against the shoulder that contact with her had made soggy.

"Think so?" he murmured, his voice distracted.

Raising her head, she searched his face curiously and found his eyes trained on her breasts. She looked down and saw the results of a cool breeze and thin, wet satin.

He lowered his head slowly and she shivered as she felt his teeth gently teasing the hardened nipples through the fabric of her gown.

"Let's go home," he whispered against her breasts.

"Yes," she murmured, her head sagging back weakly. Warmth began spreading outward from his caressing mouth, taking away the chill of the night. *Lord*, she thought wildly, as his mouth moved up her neck, *if he doesn't stop soon, I'm going to start steaming.*

Suddenly her head snapped upright as she was struck by a very uncomfortable thought. "Is there a gate in the wall around this garden?" she asked quickly.

"Yes," he said, raising his head, but before she could sigh in relief, he continued, "but they always keep it locked."

She closed her eyes briefly. "I should have known. So now what?"

"So now we make an exit that will have them talking for months," he said, chuckling, and began to walk back toward the mansion.

"Sam," she gasped. "We can't walk through the ballroom like this."

"Sure we can. Just keep your chin up and make them think it's very déclassé to appear at a ball dry." With that ridiculous statement, he stepped through the French doors, their entrance corresponding predictably with the orchestra's coffee break.

It seemed to Angie that every eye in the huge room was trained on them in the growing silence and she had to suppress a semihysterical giggle when she heard the squish of Sam's shoes as he strode casually forward.

"Lovely party, isn't it?" he said to a wide-eyed matron as they passed.

"Let's get together for lunch."

"The committee really outdid themselves on the decorations, didn't they?"

And so on as they walked through the sea of gaping people, while Angie, her hands clasped behind his neck, smiled and nodded with regal hauteur.

As the gargantuan double doors closed behind them, Sam's laughter rang out, filling the night with its deep, rich sound.

It continued when his car pulled to a halt in front of the entrance and as he handed the valet a folded bill—after he had carefully placed her soggy person in the passenger seat—and almost started anew when he glanced across at her as he slid into the driver's seat.

She leaned back in the seat and watched him curiously as his laughter died down. "Sam," she said slowly. "Did I or did I not see flash bulbs going off just before we walked out?"

He shook his head up and down, the laughter threatening to spill over once again.

"Then why are you laughing?" she asked, gritting her teeth in exasperation. "You're going to be plastered all over the newspapers tomorrow—soaking wet!"

Again his head bobbed up and down, his shoulders shaking helplessly.

"Sam!"

"Angel, it was wonderful," he gasped. "I haven't had so much fun in years."

Grasping his shoulder, she leaned forward and pushed him back in the seat. "Sam . . . darling . . . watch my lips," she said tightly. "I embarrassed you tonight. If there was one person present that I didn't offend, it wasn't from a lack of effort on my part. And except for the impromptu swim, it was all intentional. Doesn't that mean anything? Can't you see what I was doing?"

"You were being yourself," he said, sobering. "And that doesn't embarrass me in the least." He pulled her into his arms. "You were the most beautiful, vibrant, intelligent woman there tonight. I was so proud of you." He laughed softly, dipping his head to give her a brief, hard kiss. "These things are usually deadly dull, but, good Lord, you shook them up tonight."

What can I do? she thought helplessly. How can I fight a man like this? She had tried to help him—and herself—out of a situation that was potentially dangerous for them both. But, incredibly, he didn't want to be helped and defeated her at every turn.

She had hoped that they could end it in a rational way, using the facts to guide them, but it seemed now that she would have to find some other means. Some other way . . .

But as they neared his valley, the thought was replaced by one much more powerful—it could wait one more day.

Ten

Angie waved and watched as Sam's car left the parking lot, then turned and walked slowly into her apartment.

Sunday at his ranch had been a day of postponement, a leave of absence from the inevitable. Sam had watched her closely the morning before, waiting for her to renew her arguments. When she didn't even try, he had evidently decided—as she had—to hold close the little time remaining before they were forced to leave the dream behind.

But the end had come—as she had known it would—when they flew back to Dallas so she could keep an appointment with Michael Faraday.

As she walked into her bedroom to change into jeans and pick up her tape recorder, it was hard for her to summon up any enthusiasm for the coming interview. Her mind—and her heart—were still firmly held by a cool, green valley and a man with brown eyes.

"Oh swell," she muttered as she picked up her purse. "I can tell I'm going to be a tower of strength when it comes to doing without him forever."

Forever. As the bleakness of the word settled over her, she turned gratefully to the ringing telephone, stifling a pang of disappointment when she heard Patrick's voice.

"Hey, Ange," he growled. "I sure am glad you came back from wherever-you-went-that-was-none-of-my-business with whoever-you-were-with-that-I-was-also-not-supposed-to-know-about in time to make your interview with Faraday." He paused. "How was old Sam?"

"Very funny. How did you know?"

"It was a little thing all us really sharp reporters rely on. A kind of second sense—and the pictures in Sunday's paper."

"Was it awful?" she asked, grimacing. She had carefully avoided looking at the newspapers yesterday.

"No, I think it was kinda cute. You both looked like survivors of the Titanic."

"Thanks," she muttered. "Is that why you called? To let me know you thought I looked cute with goldfish in my hair?"

He chuckled. "I called to make sure you came back from never-never land in time to see our man."

"Well, I'm here so you can stop worrying." She started to hang up, then remembered something she had come across in her research. "Pat, before I left I was reading through those old underground newspapers. Did you notice anything funny about Faraday's articles after March of sixty-eight?"

"Oh, you caught that, did you?" He sounded pleased. "That's the same period he clams up about every time we talk."

"And you don't have any idea what happened?"

"Not a clue. There was a lot of activity just about then, but I haven't found anything directly related to him. You see what you can do with him today. We really need that information."

"I'll try," she said doubtfully. "Are you going to have another go at him?"

"No, I don't think so. I don't think I'll ever get any more out of him than I've already gotten. Besides he introduced me to someone who has connections all over the world. I'm going to see him tonight and get things rolling. If everything goes all right, I should be pretty busy with that from now on."

The excitement in his voice was contagious and after she replaced the phone, Angie grabbed up her purse and tape recorder and left hurriedly to keep her appointment.

She stepped out of the elevator and walked down the hall to Sam's apartment. Her movements were jerky and mechanical when she lifted her hand to ring the bell.

The door swung open seconds later and for a moment relief showed in Sam's tightly drawn features, then his gaze returned to her face. He silently studied her feverish gray eyes and the lines of pain creasing her forehead.

"Angel?" he said softly, his voice concerned.

Moving past him, she looked nervously around his apartment as though hunting for something solid to hold on to. She walked to the fireplace and picked up the figurine she had given him two weeks earlier. "I'm not late, am I?" she asked brightly.

"You said you would be here by eight. It's ten-thirty."

"Is it?" she said vaguely, moving to touch the large plant that stood in the corner of the bright, modern room. "I must—I must have lost track of the time. You know how it is when you're doing an interview." The laugh she had intended to sound carefree came out harsh and abrupt. "Did you get all your work done? You said—what was it—you said you had a meeting or something, didn't you?"

She heard him walk across the room to stand behind her, but she couldn't seem to make herself stop talking.

"Big, important, government stuff, I guess. Like what color to paint the walls of the Senate men's room." She tried to laugh again and this time it sounded even worse. "No, I guess you would have to appoint a committee for that."

"Angel," he began, placing a gentle hand on her arm.

"You know, Sam," she interrupted loudly, "I have a brilliant idea. Next time we consider entering a war, we should appoint a committee to discuss it and then the decision would never be made and we would always have peace."

He turned her around sharply and pulled her into his arms, his large hand pressing her face into his shoulder.

A terrible shudder shook her body and her eyelids drifted down wearily over the tears that suddenly filled her eyes. She leaned against him for a moment in exhaustion, then pulled out of his arms and turned away.

"Guess what?" she said, walking to the purse that she had dropped on the couch to pull out a cigarette. She lit it with fingers that shook, drew on it deeply, then continued. "I've changed my mind."

"Changed your mind?"

"About marrying you, silly." Her eyes darted around the room nervously, assiduously avoiding his. "And I think we should do it as soon as possible."

"Why?"

The quietly spoken word was like a shout in the still room. She stubbed out the cigarette and turned to face him, still not quite meeting his eyes. "Well, for lots of reasons." She moistened her dry lips. "I—I know I haven't told you, Sam, but I love you." This time she was able to meet his eyes as she spoke, for it was the simple truth.

"Yes, I know." His hands were shoved in the pockets of his gray slacks, pulling them tight across his thighs, as he stood and stared at her intently. "I've known for a long time. Why is it now sufficient reason for you to marry me?"

"It's simple really," she said earnestly, willing him to understand. "The only drawback before was my career. I know I tried to shock your friends the other night, but I'm diplomatic enough to hold my tongue when I have to. I was trying to show you what would happen if I were totally honest with people. Because I couldn't be less than honest and forthright where my work is concerned. I would have to tell the truth as I see it."

"I understand that. So what has changed?"

"Don't you see?" She swallowed nervously and stared down at her hands. "That problem doesn't exist any more because—because I've decided I don't want to be a writer anymore."

Her extraordinary statement was greeted by a tense silence.

A short, wild laugh escaped her as the silence grew heavy. "Aren't you going to say something?"

He walked the few steps to stand beside her, then pulled her down to sit with him on the couch, taking both her hands in his. "Something happened when you were interviewing Faraday," he said gently. "Tell me about it, Angel."

A sigh that was almost a whimper passed her lips as she leaned her head back against the couch. When she spoke, her voice came out in a strange monotone.

"When I first went to work for Mac, I thought I could handle anything. I wasn't exactly a rookie; I had been a reporter for eight years. But I found out my first week on the job how very, very wrong I was. The paper was doing a series of articles on child abuse and when Mac sent me out to interview a woman in jail, I was so excited to be included in the series, the facts of the case didn't really sink in."

She paused for a moment, remembering, then continued. "I walked into that depressing little room confident that I would go back with nothing less than an award-winning story. The woman was sitting quietly beside a window, her hands folded very properly in her lap." She paused thoughtfully. "Her hair was brown. I can still see it if I close my eyes. Not a rich, dark brown. Just plain, lifeless brown. She had it pulled back on her neck and secured with a rubber band—a green rubber band."

Angie knew she was trying to put off telling him everything, but suddenly the small details seemed vitally important.

"When she turned to look at me, she smiled shyly. The smile looked sincere, but her eyes didn't wrinkle at the corners. It had an odd effect on her face. An eerie effect. But I don't think I thought so at the time, so it may be that what happened later colored my memories of her." She sighed. "Anyway, I sat down beside her and told her who I was and why I wanted to talk to her—even though I knew she had been informed of the facts and had consented to the interview. It seemed only polite."

Now came the part that still brought nightmares and Angie had to force herself to go on. "She told me how the day in question began. How she had had an argument with her husband before he left for work—about the button missing on his jacket. It had left her in a bad mood. From what she told me it wasn't a good marriage, but she seemed to genuinely care for him. After he left the house, everything began to go wrong. She knocked over an ashtray in the living room and the vacuum cleaner wasn't working properly so she had to try to sweep up the ashes, but they left a gray spot on the carpet. It was new carpet and she was afraid of what her husband would say. Then things just kept getting worse. All minor things—an argument with the next-door neighbor about her dog, things like that. And through it all, her son . . ."

Angie licked her lips nervously as her eyes took on a hunted look. "Her two year old kept getting into things—the way kids that age do." Her smile was twisted and tremulous. "It's funny. As well as I remember the way she looked, it's still her voice that is freshest in my mind. It was soft and her sentences kind of trailed off at the ends in a vague, indecisive way as though she never really ended a thought.

"Tell me, Angel." The words were quiet and gentle, but a command nonetheless.

She cleared her throat. "All day the frustration kept building up in her," Angie whispered. "Nothing went right. And she had scolded the baby so many times that he was irritable too, and cried constantly, hanging on to her legs as she tried to do her housework. Her head was pounding and she couldn't think straight. And the baby kept screaming. She . . ." Angie closed her eyes tightly. "She sat down, pulled him between her knees. She put one hand on the back of his head, the other over his mouth." Her words were coming out now in frantic, ugly gasps. "She could still hear his muffled screams through her hand, but it didn't hurt her head as much, so she held her hands on him until . . . until he stopped screaming."

When Angie pulled away from the nightmare some time later, she found her face was pressed tightly against Sam's chest, his arms holding her fiercely as he rocked her back and forth.

"I'm sorry, Angel," he murmured, soothing her. "I'm so sorry."

She looked up at him unaware of the tears that

shone in his brown eyes. "She kept saying 'I just wanted him to be quiet' over and over again and her soft voice sounded like a scream inside my head. It still sounds like a scream."

She rested against his hard chest, drained of all emotion, listening to the soft voice that sounded pained and raw as it comforted her. "That's why Mac wouldn't give me any real news to cover. He was afraid I would run into something like that again."

"When he as good as told me that he couldn't trust me to be objective, I knew I had to do something. Then Pat appeared like a good fairy and offered me a chance to work on his book. I thought all my problems were solved." She sighed and moved her face against his soft shirt. "I should have known better."

Glancing up, she said, "Do you remember that night Faraday gave his talk? How his mind seemed to slip away just before the fight?" He nodded. "That's what happened every time we tried to get him to talk. We finally figured out that it happened most often when we asked questions about one period in his life—March of sixty-eight. That was right before the Chicago trouble. Several other incidents took place that month, but nothing that related directly to Faraday as far as we knew.

"Earlier today, when I got to his apartment, he seemed different somehow. More open. I found out later that he had taken something—a drug of some sort—and he was more relaxed. He could talk more easily about the past. He started to tell me about a friend of his. A former student."

She shifted her position and raised her hand to

rub the aching back of her neck. "You knew he was once a professor of sociology?"

"Yes, I had heard that." Sam's large hand took over from hers and she leaned her head forward, groaning as he eased the tension.

Glancing up through her fringe of hair, Angie said, "This particular friend had been a soulmate of Faraday's almost from the first day they met. He laughed today about some of the wild, foolish things they did together and the way they would stay up all night just talking." She gave a shaky laugh. "You know, I think I was beginning to like him. I asked him if his friend—Grady was his name—had been with him during his early activist days and that started him off again. He talked about how exciting it had been and how Grady had been right beside him through all of it . . . until March of sixty-eight."

"I knew as soon as he said it that I had hit on the reason for his strange withdrawals. Something had happened to Grady that caused this man to change completely. We knew, of course, that part of the change could have been due to heavy drug use, but it was too abrupt for it to have been that alone."

"And did you find out what happened?" Sam asked. He had turned her around and was now working on the muscles in her shoulders.

"Oh yes," she said wearily. "I asked him where Grady was now and he said very simply that he was dead. I didn't have to ask any more questions. Once he had said those words, the rest just seemed to spill out. As though it were all beyond his control. He said on the night Grady died they were both in an old abandoned factory. They were living there, but they were also using it to manufacture explosives—and hallucinogenics. Faraday had stayed up late working on an article he was writing and Grady was just relaxing. He—Grady— had taken something. Faraday still doesn't know what it was, but suddenly things started happening. He looked out the window and the yard below was swarming with police. He grabbed his notes and pulled Grady into a small storeroom that was hidden by a pile of empty boxes.

"He could hear the police entering the room that held their equipment and he turned to Grady to explain that they would wait until things died down, then try to sneak out. But Grady was out of it completely. He had no idea what was happening."

She turned around and looked up at Sam, her lip twitching nervously. "After all the noise died down, he could hear only two voices. He decided to wait another half hour, then try to get both of them out of there." She hesitated. "That's when Grady started acting strange. He had been quiet and still until then, kind of huddled up in the corner next to an old cot. Suddenly he started mumbling and his body began to jerk violently. He would clasp his hands to different parts of his body as though he were being stung. He started getting louder and Faraday tried to talk to him, begging him to keep silent."

"You don't have to finish, Angel," Sam interrupted, his voice sounding anxious and somehow angry. "I think I can guess what happened next."

"It doesn't matter. Even if I don't say it out loud, it will still be in my head." She took a deep, shaky breath. "It was all simple really. When Grady got louder and started to fight Faraday, he picked up a pillow from the cot—one of those old ones with the striped cover. The material had rotted through in one place and the feathers were spilling out. He took it and pushed it down over his friend's face."

Sam groaned as she smiled up at him. "You know what he said, Sam? He said, 'I just wanted him to be quiet.' "

She lay against him for a moment, letting him stroke her silver hair with a trembling hand. "So you see, I still can't be objective. I *cannot* calmly state those facts. I may as well take up describing the interiors of houses, like Louise, because I have failed miserably at this. I don't think I could even try it again, Sam."

Turning her head to kiss his hand, she murmured, "I meant it when I said I love you. I don't want to be anything more than your wife."

She felt him stiffen, then suddenly he stood up and began to pace.

"What's wrong, Sam? I thought you would be pleased."

"Pleased!" he said violently, stopping to stare at her, anger flaring in his brown eyes. He ran a hand through his hair in agitation, then took a deep breath and spoke calmly. "I'm sorry, but I can't do that."

"You can't?" she said, shaking her head in confusion. "You don't want to marry me?" The pain was making its way to her gray eyes. "Then it was all a lie. Why? What could you possibly gain?" As she rose from the couch, the words came pouring out of her. "We were already sleeping together, so it couldn't be that. What is this? Is it some kind of weird game you play?"

"Angel!" he shouted, his hand whipping out to grasp her arm painfully.

"You lousy bastard," she spat out in a vicious whisper, too overwrought to think straight. "Why? Why did you . . ." Her voice broke and the rest of her words were barely audible. "Why did you do it, Sam?"

Groaning deeply, he put his arms around her and held her trembling body. "Let me explain, Angel. You know you don't believe all those things you said. I handled it badly, but"—he gave a shaky laugh—"if you knew what was going on in my head, you'd understand. You threw me for one gigantic loop, babe."

He placed his hand gently on her cheek and raised her head. "Angel, I can't let it happen this way. Don't you see? I've never wanted you to give up your writing. You were the one who put that stumbling block in our way." He paused. "You were the one who said if you quit, you would never know whether it was because you loved me or because you had failed."

"But you know I love you."

"And I love you. That's why I can't let you do this to us. I can't let you use me as a way out of this. If you give up now, you won't be complete. Your writing is part of you. Angel, I don't want you to throw away that part. I want all of you."

His eyes searched hers. "It wouldn't work. You know it wouldn't. And, selfishly, I want you to come to me because you can't be without me, not because you're hiding from something and see me as a refuge."

He pushed her head back to his shoulder and

took a deep, painful breath. "You would be cheating yourself and you would be cheating me."

Pulling back, she looked up at him helplessly. "So what am I supposed to do now?"

"I can't tell you what to do, Angel. And if you weren't so upset you wouldn't even ask me to," he said quietly. "I've already pushed you too much. This is something you have to think out on your own."

He turned away and walked to the window, staring out at the lights of Dallas. "I have to go back to D.C. tomorrow. Something unexpected has come up. It will probably be at least a month before I can get back. Maybe you could use the time to think things over—without my interference."

It was all too much. Everything seemed to be falling apart. Couldn't he see how desperately she needed him? "Cast adrift," she murmured vaguely. She suddenly felt so lost and alone, even though he was standing not ten feet away. It was an emptiness she had never felt, as though her own soul had walked out on her.

She thought suddenly of a line she had read years before. It had seemed melodramatic then. Now it was as though she had written it. " 'There's a hole in my soul and all the beauty is leaking out,' " she whispered.

"Damn it, Angel," he growled, grabbing her to give her a shake.

She hadn't heard his approach and looked at him—curiously detached—as he spoke.

He buried his face in her neck and his voice grew husky with emotion as he pressed her tightly against him. "You're killing me, Angel. Lord, if you only knew how hard I tried to convince myself that I'm all you need to make you happy. But it's a lie and we both know it. This is not the end. We'll work it out if it takes the rest of our lives. And this can be a beginning if you'll let it. All you have to do is stop and think things through. Something has been keeping you from making a commitment. If it really is your work that's stopping you, then we need to work it out beforehand. There will be times that you'll be tempted to pass over a controversial subject because of me. You've got to make up your mind from the beginning that you won't let that happen. Because if you do, you'll end up hating yourself—and me for putting you in that position in the first place."

"I told you I don't want to write."

"And I don't believe you. You're tired and hurt and the thing with Faraday is too fresh in your mind. It won't be two days before you change your mind."

She pulled out of his arms. "All right. Suppose you're right about that? I'm not saying you are, but suppose. How can you be so objective about it? We're talking about something that could affect you. Why do you want it for me so much?"

He smiled. "At one point, I thought about giving up politics if it meant I could have you. Would you have wanted that?"

"No!" she gasped. "Of course not. How can you even ask? You love your work. It's a part of you. . . ." Her voice trailed off as she caught his meaning. "Sam, can we truly work it out?" She shook her head. "I'm so confused."

"You're exhausted, sweetheart. Don't even try to think about it until tomorrow when your mind is clearer. Then you'll see that it can and will work out."

"You sound so positive," she muttered irritably. "It must be nice to always be so sure of yourself."

"Babe, I'm scared to death," he said, laughing softly. "But one of us has to stay sane."

"Why does it always have to be you?" she said drily. "When is it my turn to be the sane one?" She looked up at him, her face changing. "Will you call me while you're in Washington?"

"I don't think so, Angel. I would be too tempted to try to influence you and these are decisions you have to make on your own."

"You keep saying that," she said. "I don't even know if I'm fit to make a decision." She walked reluctantly to the couch to pick up her purse. "Right now I don't think I could decide between a grape or orange popsicle."

"Don't push it," he said, his body suddenly still as he watched her walk toward the door. "Don't even think about it until you feel stronger."

How can I not think about it? she thought as she reached for the doorknob. This is my life we're talking about. She felt totally, completely abandoned. She needed his warmth and his strength tonight. She needed him.

Turning the knob slowly she pulled the door open, then irresistibly looked over her shoulder at him, a silent plea written in her gray eyes.

With urgent strides he crossed the floor and slammed the door shut, pulling her back into his arms, crushing her lips hungrily beneath his.

"Just one more night," he growled. "One more night with you."

Her trembling hands pulled at his shirt in her desperate need to feel his warmth next to her. She arched into him wildly, moaning in ecstasy when he pushed her knit shirt up over her breasts and dipped his head to latch fiercely with his ravenous mouth onto one taut nipple.

They fell together onto the plush carpet and there, before the door, came together with a savage intensity that left them drained.

The separation facing them, the instability of their future, had them turning to each other all through the night. When he walked her to her car in the pale, gray dawn, they were both light-headed with exhaustion.

After Angie had unlocked her car door Sam turned her again into his arms, holding her tightly to him. His eyes were filled with a rough kind of desperation when he finally released her. "Goodbye Angel," he whispered.

Eleven

And it seemed that he had really meant goodbye.
Angie stayed holed up in her apartment for two
endless weeks, pacing the floor like a caged
panther, thinking of the weather, the hole in her
couch—everything except the future and Sam and
her work.

And in all that empty time, except for a call
from Patrick, the telephone was silent. The mail
carrier brought only bills, and one circular an-
nouncing an annual aluminum-siding sale.

She had promised Sam she would let her brain
rest, but as she looked through the circular for
the fifth time carefully studying the prices, it suddenly occurred to her that it might have atro-
phied from disuse.

Her lethargy continued until thirteen days after
Sam's departure. She was lying on her stomach

on the floor, watching television with mindless concentration as she tried to decide who on the soaps was sleeping with whose husband, when the doorbell rang.

"Lord, Angie," the short redhead said as Angie opened the door for her. "You look tragic. What have you done to your hair?"

Angie lifted a hand to her disheveled hair. "Nothing."

"Well, maybe that's it then. You certainly *need* to do something."

"What do you suggest?" Angie asked drily. "Reseeding?"

But her humor literally went over her neighbor's head as Diane walked past her into the living room. "I could give you an introduction to Charles. He always performs miracles on my hair. And I always leave his salon feeling pampered and renewed. English accents have that effect, don't you think?"

"Diane," Angie said in exasperation. "Did you come here for any particular reason or did you just want to talk about the Monty Python of the hair set?"

"Oh!" she said. "Your mail. I picked it up along with mine to save you the trip."

She handed Angie the small stack of mail, then watched as her friend leafed through it.

When Angie came to the neat, cream envelope, her heart pounded crazily in her chest. "Diane," she said urgently. "I think I heard water running in your apartment a while ago. You didn't leave the bathroom faucet on again, did you?"

"No, of course not," Diane said in bewilderment.

"Then it must be a busted pipe. You'd better go check on it before the whole building is flooded."

Angie shoved her protesting friend out the door, then walked to the couch, staring down at the letter. Tearing open the envelope with trembling fingers, she carefully smoothed out the single sheet, postponing the reading for as long as possible—partly because she was irrationally afraid it was the final goodbye, partly because she wanted to linger over the closeness she felt as she touched Sam's stationery.

Eventually curiosity got the upper hand and she lifted the letter. Dearest one, it said in his strong, clean handwriting and her heart began to pump furiously. It was some time before she could go on to the next words.

I know I said I wouldn't get in touch with you, but I felt I had to say something about your feelings of failure after your encounter with Faraday. Angel, you shouldn't be so hard on yourself. You have very strong emotions and are deeply sensitive to human suffering—even though you try to deny it. You shouldn't hide that sensitivity. It's a beautiful part of your character. Have you ever considered the possibility that in this case it isn't necessary that you be totally objective? Why shouldn't the world feel the horror you felt when you found out about Faraday's poor friend? Let it come through in your writing, Angel, and you'll have a more honest book. Remember, babe, my love is with you even when I'm not.

Sam

Angie slowly folded the letter, then opened it again and read his words more slowly.

His love was with her. Even though she had tried to keep him out of her mind, she had never stopped feeling his love surrounding her. And at night when she had no control over her mind, he persistently starred in her dreams.

But she hadn't felt the presence of her work. Patrick's call had been to tell her that Michael Faraday had disappeared. He must have realized just what he had revealed to her and was taking no chance on being arrested.

Patrick had gone to the police with the information, telling them that it was he who had heard Faraday's confession. Of course, if Faraday were ever caught, Angie herself would have to come forward with the truth, but for now she was only too willing to let her friend answer the questions.

Shirking that duty hadn't bothered her in the least. Putting her work completely out of her mind hadn't bothered her. But now Sam's letter was pointing her in a direction she was not sure she was ready to follow.

He was wise. He had found the only possible approach to the problem. But was she a good enough—a dedicated enough—writer to feel that much emotion and have it come through in her work without destroying her? Sam had a lot more faith in her than she did in herself. Because the thought of listening again to the tape of Michael Faraday's distraught confession, and then setting the story down on paper, terrified her.

So what was she to do? There were so many things to think about. So many problems to tackle. How could she possibly solve them when her mind, heart, and body were so wrapped up in missing Sam?

"Think, Jones," she ordered desperately. "Think logically. What comes next? You've got to do what comes next."

Then, as she sat quietly on the old-fashioned couch, with the sun streaming in the window and adding diamond highlights to her silver hair, she knew what had to be done.

Sam would never accept that she wasn't running until she could prove that she had overcome her punishing desire to drop the whole Faraday thing. She had to tell the story of his friend Grady in her own words. She had to set down the tale of horror, letting the force of her feelings come through in order to purge herself of the nightmare. In order to convince Sam that she really and truly needed him for himself.

She walked slowly into her bedroom, crossed the pale green carpet, and stopped in front of the closet door. She stood for a moment, chewing the inside of her jaw, then drew in a deep, shuddering breath when she knew the moment could be put off no longer. Dragging a small chair in front of the open door, she climbed on it and reached far back into the corner of the shelf to pull out the shoebox containing her tape recorder.

This she carried to the kitchen, holding it gingerly as though it contained a bomb with a sensitive detonator. After placing it on the table, she carefully arranged her typewriter and typing paper on the table beside it, postponing the confrontation for as long as possible.

Eventually she knew she could postpone it no

longer and she sat down, switching on the small recorder with a look of fear in her gray eyes.

Describing the death of the unknown Grady was the hardest thing she had ever had to do in her life. While the afternoon wore on she sat typing, sometimes with tears streaming down her face, occasionally stopping as her body was wracked by sobs of pain and regret and anger for the young life that had been so silently and easily extinguished. She felt the terror and confusion he must have felt at the end. She felt a deep, piercing pain that in a world of so many inhumanities, this particular inhumanity would be shrugged off as insignificant. People didn't seem to understand that every act of cruelty perpetrated by a human being affected every other human being, because each act was done by a brother against a brother. The tragedy of Cain was reenacted a million times a day.

All these things she recorded on the pristine white paper. She poured out her pain and demanded answers from the reader. Even a sudden thunderstorm that blew up late in the day didn't touch her in her intense shell, and it was ten o'clock at night when she pulled the last sheet of paper from the typewriter and stacked it neatly with the rest.

Then she shoved the typewriter out of the way and dropped her head weakly into her crossed arms. It was done. She felt drained and numb, but in a tiny corner of her brain exhilaration was creeping in. Because Sam had been right: she had approached the story in her own way and deep down she knew it was good, probably the finest piece of writing she had ever done.

Stretching her aching back, Angie put away the typewriter and the tape recorder, then minutes later crawled into bed, knowing she would sleep more soundly than she had in two weeks.

The next morning, as she walked down the street, listening to the early morning sounds and inhaling the clean, early morning air, she thought about what she had accomplished the night before. She felt completely confident in her work for the first time in her life. That confidence should have brought a bounce to her steps, but they were thoughtfully slow as she walked aimlessly.

The pride she felt in her work didn't bring the expected joy. In fact it seemed to make her other problem loom larger. She had been ready to give up her career when she thought she had failed again, but Sam had been wise enough to know that she was coming to him for the wrong reasons. Now that failure had been wiped out, she knew she had to write.

But she also knew that not only this need had held her back in her relationship with Sam. Her reasons were much more complex than that, and had to do with her own feelings of self-worth. She wasn't ashamed of who or what she was. She was very simply afraid that what she was, was wrong for Sam.

In her eyes they seemed to be on opposite sides of the fence. She was average; he was exceptional. He was a success; she had just barely avoided her umpteenth failure. He was so confident; she was a cockeyed bundle of neuroses. He calmly calculated every move; she was brash and impetuous.

"He likes Doonesbury and I prefer Broom Hilda,"

she said aloud in frustration. "Lord, I'm going crazy."

She shoved her hands into her jeans and began to walk faster. She was beginning to sound sorry for herself and she didn't like it one bit.

"He's a grown man," she muttered. "He should know what he wants. And he wants *me*."

She caught the wary eye of a man passing her on the sidewalk and muttered, "Who asked you?" giving him a fierce look as she turned around to walk back in the direction of her apartment.

If only she were more sure of herself. More sure of the future. Sam was headed straight for the White House. It had already been predicted by the experts. Could she handle that? Could she live her life—raise the children she had always assumed would be in her future—in that kind of environment? And most importantly, how would Sam's future be affected by marriage to a world-class klutz?

And here she met the heart of her problem. It seemed almost certain that she would bring his career crashing down around him if she allowed herself the luxury of loving him. Because all the love in the world—and she had all the love in the world for Sam—would not make her an acceptable mate in the eyes of his adoring public.

Sam. How she ached for him. Were her doubts valid or was she letting this thing inside her push her into missing out on something that would never come her way again?

There was no way to answer that question. The only way to find out was to marry him and see what happened. Only then it would be too late; the damage would already be done.

When hunger finally quickened her steps, she was no closer to a solution than she had been in the beginning. She bent wearily to pick up the newspaper that lay on her doorstep and let herself into her apartment, tossing the paper down on the couch as she passed it on her way to the kitchen.

Later as she sat on the couch, relaxing with her last cup of coffee, she picked up the newspaper, and unfolded it before her on the coffee table.

Suddenly the coffee cup dropped to the floor, spreading a dark stain across the pale carpet while Angie clutched her stomach as though the breath had been knocked from her.

There on the front page beneath the headline that declared, SENATORS CHARGED IN BRIBERY SCANDAL was Sam's picture along with two of his well-known colleagues.

She frantically scanned the article, then closed her eyes weakly. There had to be a mistake. It stated that several senators had been approached with fake bribes and although she didn't find his name in her quick search, it was obvious from the pictures they believed these three men had accepted the bribes.

Angie jumped up and ran to the bedroom, dragging her overnight case from the closet without pausing to ask herself what she could possibly hope to accomplish in Washington. She only knew that Sam needed her and she had to go to him.

There was no question now of whether she was right for him. Right or wrong, she belonged at his side.

She threw a change of clothes and her night things into the bag with careless haste, then grabbed up her purse and raced for the door as the phone began to ring.

"Lord, Pat. Not now," she muttered in distraction as she walked out the door, ignoring the persistent ring.

The trip to the airport was a study in frustration. She had managed to hit the heart of the lunch-hour traffic, and her nerves screamed at the crawling pace as every car slowed to view a stalled car on the side of the freeway. And once she arrived at the airport, there was an hour wait before she could get a flight to Washington.

Eventually she walked on to the plane and fell thankfully into a window seat, breathing deeply to calm herself for the long flight ahead. Normally she was nervous about flying, but today she was so preoccupied with thoughts of the newspaper story that she wouldn't have noticed if the pilot had come screaming down the aisle in terror. Sam's dear face loomed before her as every passing minute took her closer to him.

When the plane landed at National, she found her luck was determined to remain bad. Every obstacle that could be dreamed of was thrown in her way, as though the gods were testing her to see just how much she wanted to get to him. By the time she got out of the terminal she was in a state of frustrated fury, and didn't even blink when she was forced to shove a man the size of a line-backer out of the way in order to confiscate his cab.

On the way to Sam's apartment she sat on the edge of her seat, cursing the traffic under her breath, bringing riotous laughter from the good-natured cab driver. She grinned at him suddenly as the adrenaline raced through her body, readying her for the fight she was prepared to have with every soul in her nation's capitol in order to clear Sam's name.

When the cab pulled to a stop, she handed the driver an indeterminate amount of money, waving goodbye when he shouted "Go to it, killer!"

Only when she entered the lobby of the hotel where Sam kept a suite of rooms did it occur to her that if he were not alone, she was going to look a little peculiar walking into his suite with an overnight bag. She hastily stashed it behind a velvet couch and walked on without pause.

She shared the elevator with three men who exited on Sam's floor in front of her. When they knocked at his door and were allowed to enter, she casually strolled in behind them, then blinked as she took in the chaos around her.

People were packed into the room like sardines, and when she saw the flashbulbs popping she knew who they were. The bulk of the crowd seemed to be concentrated in one corner of the room and she began to push through the mass of eager bodies, knowing automatically who was at the heart of the clamoring crowd. A few well placed kicks made her passage easier, and with a mighty shove she finally broke through, almost losing her balance with the effort.

The man whose back she had abused gave a yelp of pain and Sam turned in her direction, his eyes widening in surprise and a joy that took her breath away.

"Senator Clements," she shouted over the noise. "Senator, I . . ." Suddenly no words would come out and she simply stared at him, moistening her lips nervously.

"Yes, Jones?" he said, moving toward her, his eyes sparkling with love.

"Senator," she said, holding her body stiff as it began to tremble at the sight of him. "You promised me a private interview."

His eyes crinkled with laughter, his lip twitching slightly as he said, "Why, yes, I guess I did at that." He held her eyes for a moment before turning to the curiously silent reporters. "Ladies and gentlement, I find I have a previous appointment, so why don't we break for dinner and meet back here in two hours?"

"Senator . . ."

"Senator Clements!"

"I'll answer all your questions after dinner," he said firmly, then stood watching as his assistant ushered the reporters out and then followed them into the hall.

The quiet closing of the door behind Sam's assistant coincided with Angie's flight into Sam's arms. He held her to him tightly, crushing her lips beneath his.

Long moments later, he lifted his head and stared down into her misty eyes. "You know, don't you?" he whispered huskily.

"Of course I do. That's why I came," she said vehemently. "I can't believe those vultures are hanging around your door." She conveniently forgot that until a few weeks earlier she had been one of those vultures. "I'd like to flatten them all. How can they think . . ."

"Angel," he interrupted. "What are you talking about?"

She looked up at him in surprise. "I'm talking about those mangy sons of—" She stopped suddenly as it struck her that something wasn't quite right. "What did you mean when you said I knew?"

"We'll get back to that later," he hedged. "Right now I want to know why you're so angry."

"Why?" she squeaked. "I can't believe you're even asking. I'm angry because of that damned story in the paper. I'm angry because it's necessary for you to defend your name. I can't believe anyone could seriously believe you would take a bribe. My Lord, you're Honest Sam. If Diogenes had met you, he could have thrown away his lamp and retired. Those vicious, blood-sucking bastards." She glared at him suddenly, pulling away from him to pace the floor, gesturing wildly. "And I think I'm a little angry because you're taking this so coolly. There is a limit to this calm, sane bit. Get mad at them for heaven's sake!"

He sat casually on the arm of a chair and watched her pace. "You're swearing, Angel," he said softly.

She stopped and stared at him incredulously. "You want to hear swearing? Get them back in here and I'll show you swearing."

He chuckled lazily. "You know that when you swear, you have to pay the consequences."

"Sam, what in hell is wrong with you? How can you be so nonchalant?"

"Keep going, sweet. I've stored up a lot of punishment for you in the last two weeks."

She walked to the other side of the room, then back, tugging thoughtfully at her ear. "You're not the least bit worried about all this," she said, waving her hand at the door. "That means you've either gone completely off your gourd or you know something I don't."

"Well . . ." he drawled with exasperating slowness. "I gather from what you've said that you saw the pictures in the *Star*, but didn't bother to read the story."

"I glanced through it," she said, eyeing him suspiciously. "What did it say?"

"The story—and the fine print under my picture—explained that the FBI had used me in a limited way to wrap up the case."

"Then why in hell did they put your picture up there with the others?" she shouted. "Anyone passing by a newsstand would think the same thing I did."

"Angel, my sweet, you are running up one heck of a bill," he murmured, laughing softly. "I tried to call you as soon as I found out. But of course I never dreamed you wouldn't read the article. They made a mistake. It's as simple as that. The owner called this morning to apologize personally."

"And so he should," she stated belligerently, then suddenly her anger drained away, leaving only overwhelming, knee-weakening relief. "Oh Sam," she whispered.

"Come here, Angel," he said softly. "You owe me." When she stepped closer, he pulled her into his arms and suddenly he wasn't calm anymore as he collected the sweetest debt she would ever have to pay.

His mouth devoured hers, ravaging her, frantically tasting every crevice as though to reassure himself that all the sweetness still belonged to him.

She grasped his shoulders as her need rose to match his, moaning in pleasure when his lips slid to her neck.

"It's been years," he said hoarsely, his words

muffled against her soft skin. "I was beginning to think that making love to you had been a mistake. Because then I knew what I was missing when I didn't have you. I would wake up in the night and reach for you, only you were never there."

He shuddered and buried his face in her hair, inhaling the scent. "Angel, I don't know if I can go through that again."

Releasing her abruptly, he moved away from her. He smiled at her and she could tell he was trying to sound casual, but the corner of his upper lip twitched just the tiniest bit and he held his shoulders stiff and straight.

"When I saw you standing here, I thought you knew finally that nothing matters as long as we're together." He drew in a deep breath. "But you came because you thought I was in trouble. Now that you know that you don't have to fight the FBI—not to mention the entire press corps—where do we stand?"

She stared at him for a moment in uncomprehending silence, then said. "We stand together, of course."

His shoulders slumped as the breath left his lungs with a harsh swiftness. He pressed his lips together tightly, giving his groan a strange animal sound, and pulled her back into his arms.

Smoothing the curls from his forehead, she looked at him in astonishment. "Sam," she said. "You knew we would work it out. You said so."

Without taking his arms away, he moved her to the couch and pulled her down with him. "I know what I said, but it was all bluff. There has not been one minute since the cave-in that I've been sure of anything where you're concerned. Oh, I guessed that you loved me, but I didn't know if you loved me enough. You seemed so willing to have things end—only because our careers conflicted. It seemed as though you didn't care enough to try and work things out. I was afraid it was just an excuse."

"You were right," she said slowly. "It was an excuse. Oh, I was worried about how we would work it out, but the real problem was more basic than that." She paused, searching his face. "Sam, if you had a debilitating disease that you knew I would catch if you came near me, what would you do?" When he started to protest, she said, "Just answer me. I'll explain later."

"I'd stay away from you."

"That's the way I felt. I felt that I would do you irreparable harm by marrying you."

"That's crazy," he said vehemently.

"I didn't think so at the time." She gave him a disgruntled smile. "You can't know what it's like. You're so confident. Everything is easy for you. Sam, I have to struggle constantly—every minute of my life. Work or play. I'm the kind of person who pulls out a new pair of pantyhose and gets them hung on a crack in the plastic egg."

He smiled at her lovingly. "Like the horse and the cave," he murmured.

"What?" she asked with puzzled eyes.

"Did I tell you that I went back to that cave?"

She shook her head in surprise, waiting for him to continue.

"I saw the tunnel you came through that day." He shuddered. "I don't know if I could have done it and I don't have claustrophobia. After I found the tunnel I looked for the place where I was buried."

Now it was her turn to shudder.

"It was all the way across the cave." His voice became harsh and tight. "You must have crawled on your hands and knees to find me."

He was silent for a moment, his hands moving up and down her back in an absent-minded but loving caress. He was staring straight ahead at a private vision and his voice was soft as he began speaking again.

"Angel, before I met you I'd never had to fight for a woman in my life. It never occurred to me that I would have to, that I would find someone important enough to fight for. Then we were trapped together in that cave and I knew I had found someone that important. I wanted you more than I've ever wanted anything." He drew in a shaky breath. "When I went back there, I knew it was more than desire. I knew then that I had to have you forever. Every time I was around you I felt like a kid who had just seen his first butterfly. Everything about you pleased me."

He swallowed hard and when he continued his voice was gruff. "Your stubborn strength amazed me time after time. That crazy horse you were trying to ride—Oh, yes, I was watching from the barn the whole time—and then those complacent bores at the fund-raiser. Nothing can stop you for long. You hike up your britches, spit on your hands, and go in head first."

He stared down into her gray eyes, his rough thumb caressing her cheek, and said softly, "Even if I didn't love you, I would still admire you more than anyone I've ever known."

She sat there, stunned, and said, "This is crazy. All those things were the reasons I felt I was wrong for you. I was afraid my . . . unconventional personality would harm you in some way."

"Harm me," he said, smiling. "No, Angel. Never."

"Well, actually," she said sheepishly, "that's what I decided. When I thought you were in trouble, all the good, logical reasons I had thought were keeping us apart seemed like just so much garbage. I sat on the plane and tore every one of those reasons to shreds."

She laughed softly. "I had told myself that if I ever married I wanted a house like Beaver Cleaver and kids and a husband who stayed around long enough to watch them grow. On the plane I tried to imagine myself married to someone who could give me those things, but the thought of spending my life with someone who was not you gave me a pain . . . here." She pressed his hand to her breast.

"Five minutes with you is worth more than years with any other man," she whispered. "And if I have to raise our kids in the White House, then we'll just have to turn the Oval Office into a nursery so you can watch them while you work."

She rubbed her face against his. "All the other reasons fell just as easily. Except one: the fact that I would never be the typical political wife—especially since I found out you were right about my writing. That one was a little tougher. Then I thought about why I was sitting on that plane. As crazy as it sounds, I was on my way to protect you. And that settled the whole thing." She looked up at him, making a face to show that she couldn't believe she hadn't thought of it earlier. "I could never harm you. I love you too much. And I'll do what I have to in order to keep you safe."

She touched his face and stared into his loving, brown eyes. "There are a lot of people out there who will try to hurt you, now and in the future. You're going to need someone who is unquestioningly, body and soul, on your side. And that's me, because no one could possibly love you the way I do."

His mouth swooped to capture the loving words on her lips and they spent the next few emotion-charged minutes trying desperately to make one body out of two. Every touch stoked a fire that was beginning to grow out of control.

"Angel?" he murmured huskily as he unfastened another button.

"M-m-m?" she whispered in distraction as his tie continued to frustrate her.

"We've already used up one-fourth of our two hours. If we don't move to the bedroom, your colleagues are going to walk in on the story of their lives."

Reluctantly she removed her hands from his neck. She stood, then moaned as the phone rang.

She heard him answer without really listening to the words. Then he turned around and gave her a look that would melt steel and said into the receiver, "Oh, by the way, Mrs. Levine. I'm switching my phone back to the office. I'll be in conference for the next hour and a half, so don't put any calls through." He grinned suddenly. "Miss Jones and I will be discussing our plans to redecorate the White House."

Twelve

"Senator!"

The tall, thin man in the first row stood up when Senator Clements pointed to him. "Bishop. Fort Worth *Daily News*," he said, identifying himself. "Senator, we've all heard the rumor that you're going to try your hand in the next presidential election. Is there any truth to that or is it just speculation?"

Angie hid her smile and stared at the man on the dais. A lock of curly, brown hair fell across his forehead and his honest farmer's face was creased by a crooked smile as he formed his answer.

Angie had never believed in the timeless love she had always read about, love that sinks everything else into the background to consume the two people involved. At least she hadn't before Sam. Now she knew that it did exist. She was living proof. She would have gladly, joyously, given up her career, her independence—her life if Sam had asked it. But he wouldn't because that was a part of the loving, too.

She could see the same devotion in his eyes. And he proved it every day. Not by any enormous sacrifice, but by the way his eyes searched for her across the room at a party. By the way, after a campaign speech, he came back to their hotel room with a desperate need for her. He seemed to draw strength from her to keep up the killing pace he maintained during these trips.

She felt herself swell inside at the thought of what he had given her in the past six years. A life—fast paced certainly—but bursting with love, filled to overflowing with passion and tenderness. Placing a hand on her gently rounded stomach, she grinned. Overflowing was certainly the word for it. The baby that was growing inside her would be born into their own perfect little piece of the world. Because Sam was right. Peace and love begin with one person, then grow to one family and one community until all the pieces interconnect.

Smiling a slow, loving smile, she remembered the day he had met the reporters, shortly after the book she and Pat had co-authored had hit the stands. She had been so afraid. She had known the moment was inevitable, even from the day they had received an advance from a publisher based solely on Pat's outline and her treatment of the interview with Faraday. She had known, but it hadn't stopped the fear.

When a member of the press had asked Sam if

he thought the book would hurt him in the election, he had turned to look at her, the love shining bright in his eyes, and said, "Personally I believe the voters will think I'm one smart bird for having married such an extraordinary woman. She and Patrick Denby took a sensational story about underground activists and turned it into a sensitive portrayal of all men's hopes and fears." He had paused then. "I'm very proud of her."

Apparently all the world loves a man who loves his wife, for he was elected by a landslide. And the love between them grew and swelled to enormous proportions, accepting each setback as it came, softening each blow.

She listened now as he denied the rumors about the next presidential election and moved on to a man who was extremely angry that a bill he supported had been defeated.

Sam looked at the man for a moment, then out into the crowd. "This government of ours is not perfect," he said quietly across the silence. "It will never be perfect. But we can't give up on it. We have to keep striving for the unobtainable goal. We have to right first *one* wrong, then one more—because the wrongs never go away. It's slow and it's frustrating, but it's the only way that works."

Angie looked around the room at the expressions on the faces of his audience. She accepted silently the fact that it wouldn't be long before he took that biggest step. These people would demand it of him. The knowledge brought mixed feelings, the strongest of which was a heart-pounding pride in her man.

As the press conference broke up she stood still and waited for the moment that still—after six years—meant so much. He began to search the milling crowd and then his eyes met hers and he was home.

BANTAM NEVER SOUNDED SO GOOD
NEW SUBLIMINAL SELF-HELP TAPES
FROM BANTAM AUDIO PUBLISHING
Invest in the powers of your mind.

Years of extensive research and personal experience have proved that it is possible to release powers hidden in the subconscious through the rise of subliminal suggestion. Now the Bantam Audio Self-Help series, produced by Audio Activation, combines sophisticated psychological techniques of behavior modification with subliminal stimulation that will help you get what you want out of life.

☐ 45106	GET A GOOD NIGHT'S SLEEP . . . EVERY NIGHT: FEMALE	$7.95
☐ 45107	GET A GOOD NIGHT'S SLEEP . . . EVERY NIGHT: MALE	$7.95
☐ 45041	STRESS-FREE FOREVER: FEMALE	$8.95
☐ 45042	STRESS-FREE FOREVER: MALE	$8.95
☐ 45081	YOU'RE IRRESISTIBLE!: FEMALE	$7.95
☐ 45082	YOU'RE IRRESISTIBLE!: MALE	$7.95
☐ 45004	SLIM FOREVER: FOR WOMEN	$8.95
☐ 45005	SLIM FOREVER: FOR MEN	$8.95
☐ 45022	POSITIVELY CHANGE YOUR LIFE: FOR WOMEN	$7.95
☐ 45023	POSITIVELY CHANGE YOUR LIFE: FOR MEN	$7.95
☐ 45035	STOP SMOKING FOREVER: FOR WOMEN	$7.95
☐ 45036	STOP SMOKING FOREVER: FOR MEN	$7.95
☐ 45094	IMPROVE YOUR CONCENTRATION: WOMEN	$7.95
☐ 45095	IMPROVE YOUR CONCENTRATION: MEN	$7.95
☐ 45112	AWAKEN YOUR SENSUALITY: FEMALE	$7.95
☐ 45113	AWKAEN YOUR SENSUALITY: MALE	$7.95
☐ 45130	DEVELOP INTUITION: WOMEN	$7.95
☐ 45131	DEVELOP INTUITION: MEN	$7.95
☐ 45016	PLAY TO WIN: WOMEN	$7.95
☐ 45017	PLAY TO WIN: MEN	$7.95
☐ 45010	WEALTH, COME TO YOU: FEMALE	$7.95
☐ 45011	WEALTH, COME TO YOU: MALE	$7.95

Look for them at your local bookstore, or use this handy page to order.

Bantam Books, Dept. BAP4, 414 East Golf Road, Des Plaines, IL 60016

Please send me _____ copies of the tapes I have checked. I am enclosing $_____ (please add $2.00 to cover postage and handling). Send check or money order—no cash or C.O.D.s please.

Mr/Ms _____

Address_____

City/State _____ Zip _____

BAP4—6/89

Please allow four to six weeks for delivery. This offer expires 12/89. Prices and availability subject to change without notice.

NEW!

Handsome Book Covers Specially Designed To Fit Loveswept Books

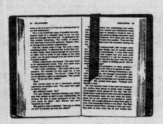

Our new French Calf Vinyl book covers come in a set of three great colors—royal blue, scarlet red and kachina green.

Each 7" × 9½" book cover has two deep vertical pockets, a handy sewn-in bookmark, and is soil and scratch resistant.

To order your set, use the form below.

BANTAM
SHOP·AT·HOME
C·A·T·A·L·O·G

Special Offer
Buy a Bantam Book
for only 50¢.

Now you can have Bantam's catalog filled with hundreds of titles plus take advantage of our unique and exciting bonus book offer. A special offer which gives you the opportunity to purchase a Bantam book for only 50¢. Here's how!

By ordering any five books at the regular price per order, you can also choose any other single book listed (up to a $5.95 value) for just 50¢. Some restrictions do apply, but for further details why not send for Bantam's catalog of titles today!

Just send us your name and address and we will send you a catalog!
